GW00761123

IN THE TENT

David Rees

IN THE TENT

LONDON : DENNIS DOBSON

For Dorothy and Tony Steer

First published in Great Britain 1979 by
Dobson Books Ltd., 80 Kensington Church Street, London W.8

Photoset by Bristol Typesetting Co. Ltd.
and printed and bound by
Robert Hartnoll Ltd., Bodmin, Cornwall

ISBN 0 234 72091 3

J'ai seul la clef de cette parade

—Rimbaud

I, like an usurpt town, to another due,
Labour to admit you, but, oh, to no end

—Donne

Beyond a wholesome discipline, be gentle with yourself.
You are a child of the universe no less than the trees and the
stars. You have a right to be here. And whether or not it is
clear to you, no doubt the universe is unfolding as it should.
Therefore be at peace with God, whatever you conceive
Him to be.

—Anon

Note

The story of the siege of Exeter in 1646 is not meant to be historically accurate in every detail. The length of the siege, for instance, was some seven months, not a matter of days, and Cromwell did not encamp his army on the west side of the river. Fairfax needed no assistance from him, and none was given. Nor did Goring blow up the Exe Bridge. Otherwise the account is as truthful as it is possible to make it: Charles I's daughter was born in Exeter and lived there throughout the siege; Goring and his men did run away during the night; the surrender was negotiated at Sir John Bampfylde's house at Poltimore; Fairfax's terms were as they are stated; the cathedral was divided in two; and the citizens suffered more from Berkeley's administration than from the Roundhead conquerors. And Fairfax claimed, despite the length of the siege, that he had captured the city without a shot being fired. The incident with the organ pipes is also true, though it occurred at a later date when the Commonwealth became more extreme in its religious attitudes. The city clergy did not long enjoy their 'special protection'. They were in fact cruelly persecuted, but that is outside the span of this story.

CHAPTER ONE

The blob on the school atlas had grown, expanded until it became a whole world. He was standing on the battlements of a city. One way a wide smelly moat, fields that undulated gently towards a river. Beyond, dark woods and a steep escarpment of hills. The other way lawns, a garden, a mansion (the Bishop's palace, presumably), the cathedral. Odd: its towers were on the transepts. A teeming, densely-populated city in medieval times. No, not medieval; there were half-timbered houses of the Tudor period, stone-built houses of a yet later date. Peoples' clothes; that would give some clue. Street-vendors shouting their wares, women buying provisions. Remarkably little for sale in the markets, everyone grumbling at high prices. Yesterday meat had been cheaper, the day before cheaper still. 'This is the last of it,' a butcher said. 'I don't mean till tomorrow, mistress. It is *the* last.' A man on horseback, frock coat, Charles I wig. The roads all muddy lanes or worn cobbles. A gutter in the centre of the street, where offal rotted and filthy water swept. Disgusting unhygienic smells; middens. People, people, too many people, refugees from outlying villages seeking sanctuary inside an impregnable fortress.

Someone came towards him along the wall. Handsome: tall, lean, a rugged face, a moustache; an air of purposefulness, of authority, in his stride. A man in his late twenties.

'Timothy Keegan?'

'Yes.'

'Follow me.' Tim obeyed. 'You know you are assigned to me?'

'Yes.'

They walked in silence. There was no more moat; in its stead a burial ground, then several houses, a Quaker meeting-place and a hospital, all in ruins, roofless and charred. From here to the river were remnants of material draped on drying-racks, useless, mildewed, ripped by the wind. It was a fine day now after long rain; October, though dull clouds dragged over the south-west hills. The drying-racks: hundreds, thousands of them. The industrial quarter, of course: a great centre of the cloth industry; a major port, but there were no ships moored at the quay in these difficult times.

They approached the massive south gate and Holy Trinity church. Church and gate were joined; the city wall was the south wall of the nave. There were two doors; one in the side of Holy Trinity tower, the other in the middle storey of the gatehouse. The man unlocked the latter, and Tim was in a room so large that it occupied the entire first floor. A slit of a window overlooked the dusty track which meandered alongside the estuary; a larger pane of glass opened on to a street where old women with pitchers clustered round a conduit and busied themselves more in gossip than in drawing water.

'We live here, you and I,' said the man. 'Eating, recreation, sleeping, all in this room. You cook, keep the place clean. Never mind the lack of food in the shops. There is plenty for us, the soldiers. When the attack comes, there will be other duties as well; that goes without saying.

Do you play chess? Oh, there is only the one bed; of course you will share it with me.'

'Thank you.' The tone of voice seemed to indicate that such an offer demanded gratitude; perhaps servants usually slept on the floor.

'Anthony Fare. Apt I suppose.' He laughed. His hair, thick, down to his neck in ringlets, was so pale it was almost albino; beautiful, Tim thought. 'Do you know me?' Anthony asked.

'I don't, yet I do. I've seen you. I can't say where.'

Anthony looked at him, probing behind the words. His eyes were blue, intense, more his modes of question and answer than was his speech. 'Whose party are you?'

'Royalist.' Tim flushed. To admit to Parliamentarian in one of the King's strongholds would hardy be politic; Royalist was the automatic response: they had right on their side, the city's authorities, even if corrupt, inefficient, repressive. Deep down he was Parliamentarian, but he hardly dared admit it even to himself, yet.

Again, the searching blue stare, and was there, perhaps, a hint of disappointment? The hint was fleeting, so suddenly switched off that Tim could not be sure. 'One has to ask,' Anthony said, non-committally. 'The city is full of Roundhead sympathizers. Understandable. It declared for Parliament in 1642, but since the last siege . . . well, you know this. Come, you must see what we have in the gate-house. You've not been in here before?'

'No.'

The upper floor was divided into two rooms. In the first, provisions: vats of cheese, beer barrels, sides of beef and ham, preserved fruits in jars. 'It is of the utmost import-ance,' Anthony said, 'that you say not a word about this to any of the populace. Not even to your parents. This is for

the army. What remains of the army,' he added, bitterly.
'Did your parents mind you coming?'

'My father's with Lord Goring's men.'

'Yes, they left last night under cover of darkness. One
thousand horse. Cowardice? Hmm. To regroup near
Okehampton, we're told. The enemy think they're still
here. But, hard on the citizens, yes? Almost no-one now to
defend them.' He led the way into the second room, the
muniment chamber he called it, full of powder, shot,
muskets; for distribution, he explained, when the time
came.

'When will the time come?' Tim asked. 'The countryside's so peaceful.' He looked out of the window at the
autumn afternoon, the green lush land, the distant sea.

'The New Model, intelligence has it, has split in two.
Fairfax held a council of war on the twenty-first, and sent
one half of his men south-west. They camped at Alphington
last night; only the weather and the mud has stopped them
reaching the river.' He pointed to the estuary. 'Tonight we
shall see them. There. Are you frightened?'

'No.'

Anthony relaxed, smiled; the eyes were friendly now.
'Sir Hardress Waller has marched the rest of the New
Model to Topsham. So we are cut off. Besieged. Again.
One morning we shall wake up and find an army ringed
round us, touching the foot of our walls. Cromwell is at
Crediton; he'll attack from the north.' He shivered. 'I'm
glad we're defending the south gate.' He climbed up a
stone spiral staircase and they were on the roof. The street
was a long way down; people were not exactly the size of
ants, but they looked frighteningly small. The gatehouse
was solid, impossible to scale, reassuring. It was higher
than Holy Trinity tower. The view was immense: hills,

estuary, sea. No soldiers in the silent fields. No-one at all. Somewhere, hidden, were Cromwell, Fairfax, Waller. Steel. Death. The city seemed little and frail. Houses were flimsy toys; the people, dolls. Only the walls all round and the four gates were imposing, protective.

When they were by the small entrance-lodge at street level, Anthony started to operate the machinery that closed the gate. The huge wooden doors banged to with a hollow boom that reverberated sadly. 'The last of the four to shut,' he said. 'We are now, officially, in a state of siege.' He looked at Tim. 'There's fear in you.' Tim nodded. 'Don't be afraid. It will be all right. Trust me.' Tim nodded again. He did. Self-knowledge, skill, experience, all there in the voice, in the body. 'We are what we are,' Anthony said, enigmatically, and led him upstairs to the living-quarters.

He looked at the blob on the map, the place where, after closing his eyes, he had stuck the compass-point. Exeter. He had never been there, nor to any place within a hundred miles of it. He gazed out of the classroom window, over the roofs of the drab town where he had lived all the seventeen years of his life, to the flat grey sea and the docks where the continental car ferries tied up; and he thought of the flat grey landscape behind the town, and the huge East Anglian sky.

The bell for the end of afternoon school had jangled at least ten minutes ago. He had dawdled, pretending to search for something in his desk. Aaron Brown was still there, talking to two other boys, John Hewitt and Ray Suñer. Aaron fascinated him. Casual and arrogant, expert on a guitar. Girls adored him. Aaron picked and chose, went with this one or that one, did not get involved. Almost certainly wanted only the one thing.

They might speak to each other if they met by accident in London or in the Sahara Desert, but not at school. Tim had never been out with a girl, had never wanted to; nor did he play games, or make coarse sexual jokes or follow pop music. He worked hard, Geography, English and History for 'A' level; Aaron idled. They had absolutely nothing in common, so why should this lord, this sungod, talk to him? It wasn't in the nature of things.

History was Tim's delight, though he wished Mr Coe would concentrate less on the battles of the Civil War, its political and religious issues. The passions of the conflict were a dead letter, impenetrable to sympathy. What did the ordinary people think; how did they cope?

The three boys, who were lounging against the blackboard, were discussing their plans for half-term. As from now school had finished; a week and two weekends of October freedom lay ahead. They had a problem. Their holiday in the Lake District—climbing Great Gable, the Langdale Pikes, Scafell, Helvellyn, Skiddaw—was in jeopardy. There should have been a fourth boy, Brian Kiddall. Brian, the expedition's cook, had flu.

'He's the only one of us who knows the mountains,' Aaron pointed out. 'My mother made her usual flap until she knew he'd been before.'

Ah! Even sungods have mothers. Tim remembered seeing her at Open Day, dumpy, unattractive, garrulous. They had obviously forgotten he was still in the classroom; or else, more likely, he was of such little significance to these kings of the school that it was of no matter he should overhear weakness.

'Don't tell her,' Ray Suñer said. Ray was interesting. Pure Spanish, Ramón his real Christian name, and there was a ~ over the n of his surname; Soonyer it was pronounced. But he was born and bred here and spoke with a thick flat Suffolk accent. His grandfather had fled his native country when the Republic collapsed. Doctor Negrín, Dolores Ibarruri, and Casares Quiroga were more familiar people to Ray than Cromwell and Charles the First.

'I don't have to tell her; that's perfectly true,' Aaron conceded. 'But Brian owns the tent. Oh, I suppose it'll work out.'

'He'll still lend it to us,' said John Hewitt, a slow easy-mannered youth with wide-apart blue eyes, the son of centuries of farm labourers now a generation removed from the land. His family was moving house soon, back to a village a few miles away. Tim knew all these details: he listened and remembered, knew where these boys lived, though he had never entered their lives. Aaron's father, for instance, owned the pub, The King's Head, on Flatsea, that island of silt and marram grass in the river estuary, one station down the line. Aaron was the third of four brothers.

'Of course it'll work out,' said Ray. 'What are you getting so steamed up about?'

'I'm not.'

'Ron thinks he'll have all the more to hump on his own shoulders,' John said.

'Well, that's it then,' Aaron decided, as if he was bringing a board meeting, or council of war, to a close. 'I don't tell her. Let's be off home out of this dump.' He moved across to his desk, shuffled through his books then banged the lid shut. It was in the front row; Tim's was at the back. 'No need to take any bloody work home, thank God!'

'It says here "Ginny loves Aaron",' said Ray, who was reading a desk-top. 'There's a bleeding heart in red biro.'

'Ginny Mason?' Aaron asked. 'She's out of luck. Flat-chested old bat.' The coarseness, as always, made Tim wince.

'No, *he* wants Mary Miller,' said John, winking at Ray.

'So I do and why not? She's gorgeous!' He outlined her shape with his hands.

Ray giggled. 'She's well beyond your class.'

'She's not. What makes you think that? I've been out with her, haven't I? I'm taking her out on Thursday, day after we come back from the Lakes.' Aaron was lost, for the moment, in his vision of it.

'How's your girl?' Ray asked John.

'All right.' John had been going steady with Lesley Fox ever since they were both fourteen. Coffee bar once during the week, disco or cinema Saturday nights, tea and television at her house or his house on Sundays. Occasionally they were seen walking out, hand in hand.

'All right! That's all you ever say, all right, all right, all right!' Ray exclaimed, suddenly heated. 'What do you do with each other? What do you say to each other?'

'Mind your own business, Franco.' But he smiled his wide farm labourer's smile, no malice.

'Let's get home,' Aaron said, picking up his bag. The other two followed him to the door.

Words in Tim's mind: Aaron, I love you. You're beautiful. Blue eyes, long blond hair (too long for teachers' comfort). All of a happy uncomplicated piece. And I'm not. No no no no no! Wrong. Wicked. I'd go to Hell; I'd be in mortal sin. Jesus, Mary, Joseph, help! I believe in the infinite mercy and goodness of God and yet there is also His most terrible anger, which justly punishes sinners. Kiss Aaron. No no no! What else with him, what else would I have him do to me? NO NO!! Jesus, Mary, Joseph, HELP!!

But they didn't. His heart beating so fast and his hands so trembling that he could hardly make himself speak, Tim said 'I'll come with you.' Why not? He had been to the Lakes before, more than once; he didn't exactly know it like the back of his hand, but he had stood on the summit of Gable, of Helvellyn, of Scafell Pike. He and his parents had been there these last three summers, to a guest-house in Wasdale under the enormous shadow of Ling Mell. And he was used to cooking too; with both his father and mother at work, he, the lone sibling, had always been a latchkey child, letting himself into an empty house after school, making his own tea.

The three boys stopped in the doorway and turned. They didn't jeer or look condescending. Just puzzled. 'Why?' Ray asked, frowning.

'Who is it?' Aaron was already out in the corridor.

'You don't live my way,' John said.

'I don't mean home. I mean . . . to the Lakes.'

'What for?' Aaron came back into the room. 'Why do you want to? You're hardly . . . well . . . Besides, we don't need anybody else.'

John stared; Ray contemplated the blackboard.

Wishing the earth would swallow him up, Tim explained about the cooking and knowing the mountains; his father would lend him any equipment they might lack. (Would he? It might be a hard job persuading his parents, and how did he propose to get to Mass on Sunday, his mother would ask; it wouldn't be like the summer, with the car: but his father, he remembered, often grumbled at him, despised him even, for not being out of doors and physical. Dad would, perhaps, allow it, after the usual nagging session.) He could be useful, he said, to the expedition; he was sure of it, and he promised not to get in their way or be a burden.

There was a lengthy argument, most of the objections coming, surprisingly, from Ray. Aaron's contributions were feeble, and eventually he was silent; looked just a little relieved in fact. The sungod's weakness. Tim, delighted and astonished, knew they would accept him.

'Oh let him come for Christ's sake!' said John, at last. 'What a fuss you cause, Ray! What harm can he possibly do us?'

Ray protested, but without force now, and he shut up altogether when Aaron said he couldn't care one way or the other. And so it was settled.

They dispersed to their homes. The Suñers' flat was on the tenth floor of a tower block near the station; John lived in one of the few houses in Balaclava Street that wasn't West Indian or bed-sit, Tim in a district of pre-war semis: discreet laurel hedges, established gardens (laburnums, flowering cherries), and ladies like his mother with decided opinions and hats. Such, he reflected as he picked privet leaves and inhaled their sweet scent, was the nature of a class at Oozedam Comprehensive.

Ray walked along with Aaron. Keegan was a weakling, a weed, a wet, a swot, he said, a pouff.

'You mean he's queer?' Aaron asked. 'How do you know?'

'He is. He'll spoil everything.'

'We did that, once upon a time.'

'That was different.' Ray was embarrassed. They were fourteen then; Saturday mornings in Ray's bedroom, listening to pop, looking at nudie magazines. It was only because of the naked women and Aaron didn't quite know then how to go out with girls; it had finished when he did.

'I'm not ashamed it happened,' Aaron said. 'Even

16

though I usually started it.' He was speaking the truth; his lack of guilt had meant their friendship wasn't spoiled.

'Nor am I.' But it was more complicated for Ray. He thought for a moment, then said, 'Tim fancies you.'

'That's his problem,' Aaron said, shrugging his shoulders.

The air was sharp with frost; ice and a few snow-streaks lay on the stones, but the four boys glowed, exulting, from the climb. Light was failing. The huge wide world falling away from the summit of Great Gable was a marvel beyond imagining. Tim could see that the planet Earth curved. The galaxies above, growing just visible, emphasised distance, vastness. The turning world; he knew it was spinning, infinitely little, infinitely enormous. At the edges, the sea. Wastwater, a steel mirror, deepest of all lakes, yet a puddle between folds. Cloud, soft cotton wool wraps of it slowly rolling over Steeple and Haycock. The colours: shadows, impossibly purple, of Illgill Head, Great End, Ling Mell; minute strips of green fields in the valleys, the lower slopes of mountains a blaze of copper ferns. Gable, an immensity of scree, grey stone, grey slate: barren, dangerous. The slopes! The depths, the heights! The sky!

Ray and John were talking geography: cols, occlusions, rifts, glaciation. 'A sunken dome,' Ray informed him. 'Scafell Pike is the centre. They're the oldest mountains in the world.' How unpoetic, Tim thought, how insensitive.

'Not a bad view,' Aaron said, glancing round for a moment, his breath steaming like a horse's after a gallop. He turned away and kicked stones as he would any time, anywhere.

'The weather won't change,' Ray said. 'That man was talking rubbish.' The sun burned on the horizon, reassuring. The air was so still you could hear it.

'That's Jupiter,' said John, pointing.

Someone from the Mountain Rescue had stopped them at Wasdale Head. They would be camping at the top of the Honister Pass near the youth hostel, they told him. That seemed satisfactory, but when he asked, and they said they would be climbing the Pikes of Langdale tomorrow, he looked doubtful: rain and low cloud was the forecast. To lose the way was easy. They intended to camp in Langdale? Yes, they replied.

'Not a bad view,' Aaron repeated, scoring a goal on the cairn. 'There's my crags.'

'What do you mean, your crags?'

'Aaron Crags. That's what they're called. Look at the map if you don't believe me.'

'There's a gully called Aaron Slack as well,' Ray said. 'Sounds more appropriate. Slack Alice.'

Evening in the tent and Tim was happy. His eyes were filled with landscape, the purple shadows. The tent, Japanese, was child's play to erect; it opened like an umbrella and was almost perfectly round. He had cooked to the others' liking, or at least there were no adverse comments. As on the train he listened to the conversation more than he contributed, the four of them sprawled on their sleeping-bags. Aaron and John smoked; Ray grumbled that he wanted booze. They worked out tomorrow's route, Seathwaite, Sprinkling Tarn, Esk Hause, Angle Tarn; easy, Tim said, the east–west motorway of the mountains, but then problems: the way to the top of the Langdale Pikes was not well defined; in cloud they might get lost.

'If there's cloud there's little point in going up them,' John said. 'There'll be nothing to see.'

So they would continue down the motorway to the camp site by the Old Dungeon Ghyll Hotel.

They listened to pop on Ray's transistor.

School, girls, football, the top thirty; back and forth the talk went round these topics, Ipswich Town, Mary Miller, Abba, idiot teachers. They played cards. Aaron pulled out a book, lost himself in *Confessions of a Window Cleaner*.

'Read out the juicy bits,' Ray suggested. But Aaron didn't.

Ray and John went outside, wandered a few yards from the tent, and fell into conversation with some boys and girls from the youth hostel. Tim, furtively, took Blake from his rucksack and hoped Aaron wouldn't ask what it was, this 'A' level set text. He was a great comfort, Blake; here were his own longings, so that while he read they lost their shame and were invested with authority.

Exuberance is Beauty. Energy is Eternal Delight. So it is, Aaron, so you are.

And Priests in black gowns were walking their rounds,
And binding with briars my joys and desires.

Me, yes, me, Tim.

He who desires but acts not, breeds pestilence.

I want permission to act. Permission? Yes, there must be permission.

Ray came running back; with great excitement said someone staying at the hostel had a minibus. There was room for the four of them; this man and some others were going down to the pub in Borrowdale. So they all piled in (Blake would always be there, later) and Tim, for the half-hour before closing-time, was in a sleepy stuffy room, full of male legs in boots, beards, ropes, pints firmly held, the pretend-man he felt he was ignored and therefore accepted. He was happy. It wasn't only the beer, he thought. Man among men. Ray chatted up a girl from the youth hostel.

19

Aaron, fancying her perhaps, or jealous of Ray enjoying himself, sulked. John, tongue loosened, talked to Tim; school again, for there was little else in common.

They slept, four heads to the centre pole of the tent. Aaron's face inches away, asleep, breathing evenly. Impossible for Tim to sleep. He had seen his love undress and hoped desperately his own eyes had gone unnoticed. Last summer's suntan on Aaron was still evident, but white where he'd worn his bathing trunks. Almost white hair on the golden legs. There was only one possible answer in the circumstances, he told himself. Aaron, stretch out a hand and touch me, put your hand where mine is! Mortal sin, the Church said. By yourself or with another; it didn't matter. The Church also said that to sin in thought was as bad as to sin in deed. So, was he in any less danger of going to Hell if he stopped? Those who restrain Desire do so, because theirs is weak enough to be restrained, Blake said. Lord Jesus Christ, help! See His face and then go on? Christ's face, Christ's face in my head, not Ron's. The beauty of him lying beside me, breathing. I am sorry, above all things, that I have offended Thee, because Thou art infinitely good, and sin is infinitely displeasing to Thee. I desire to love Thee with my whole heart, and I firmly purpose, by the help of Thy grace, to serve Thee more faithfully in the time to come.

There was a queer effeminate boy called Noel Haynes at school. Was he like nancy Noel? He hoped not.

He stopped. An achievement. Of sorts. Father Sullivan in the confessional next time would approve. He was still wide awake.

'It's not far,' said Anthony, leading him down a dark alleyway off South Street.

'Why are we going?' Tim asked.

'Officially to spy; he is said to be dangerous. Unofficially to do nothing. I doubt if I'll report anything.'

Richard Saint-Hill was a dark foreign-looking man about the same age as Anthony. He talked too much; sense drowned in sound. The meeting, of necessity, was totally clandestine, and only five people, apart from Tim and Anthony, were present. Anthony nodded to someone; the sexton of Holy Trinity, he explained when Tim asked, a young man called Jake. Saint-Hill's words, full of Biblical echoes, were a jumble of ill-digested Utopian ideas, reminiscent of some of the stranger religious beliefs the period had spawned. His theme, when he did not wander from it, was that the city was doomed. The Parliamentarian success was inevitable (and few people in Exeter, from the meanest labourer to Sir John Berkeley himself, would privately have disagreed). The only realistic course of action was to make things so easy for the Puritans that when they entered the city they would harm not a hair of the head of any man, woman or child. To this end he proposed that a small party of respected and influential sympathizers of the Parliament's cause should steal out of the city (there were many possible ways of doing this) and, in exchange for absolutely firm guarantees concerning the safety of the populace, they should reveal these secret routes to the enemy. Any conflict, any hardship would thus be avoided.

There was conviction in his voice, but his eyes did not seem to look outward; they were obsessed with some inner vision.

'What do you think of this Saint-Hill, Tim?' Anthony asked, later, when they were back in their room at the gatehouse. They were playing chess. There were three glasses of white wine on the table, and a bunch of grapes.

The third glass was for Jake who had returned with them.

'A crank? I have your bishop, by the way.'

'If you do I capture your queen. A man like that deserves no respect; he can stand up for no side at the time to count heads, and such a time has come and has been with us these four years. Men like him sell their principles for a quiet life, betray themselves for the softest option. He is, you see, a Royalist. A fanatical supporter of the King. Divine right used to be the subject with which he would drive us all to boredom and drink.'

'What do you intend to do with him?'

'Nothing. Let him and his respected merchants, if he can find any, creep away and seek out Fairfax. Sir Thomas will not, I think, welcome him with open arms. Checkmate!' Anthony laughed. 'See! I move my rook and your king is caught behind his row of pawns. Inert, ineffective little pawns! Always beware of an attack in the rear.'

'I will try,' Tim said, smiling. Jake laughed. Tim looked at him; an innocent face, yet not so innocent; wide-apart blue eyes.

Anthony poured more wine. He picked up his lute, and, sitting cross-legged on the floor, sang sad songs and madrigals:

'Draw on, sweet night, best friend unto those cares
That do arise from painful melancholy.'

'April is in my mistress' face,
And July in her eyes hath place.
Within her bosom is September,
But in her heart is cold December.'

The voice was as melancholy as the words, the music, the plaintive sob of the lute-strings. Tim watched, fascinated. He sipped the wine, ate more grapes.

'What's to come is still unsure:
In delay there lies no plenty;
Then come kiss me, sweet and twenty,
    Youth's a stuff will not endure.'

Anthony put down his lute. 'We'll see more of Saint-Hill before long,' he said. He stood up, stretching. 'Bedtime,' he announced.

Jake left. 'He doesn't say much, does he?' Tim observed. 'Who is he?'

He slept.

CHAPTER TWO

The man from the Mountain Rescue had been right. They awoke to low cloud and a thin drizzling rain. Visibility was only a few yards; even the youth hostel, a stone's throw away from the tent, had vanished. They argued over breakfast (Ray and Aaron, that is; John listened, Tim did the dishes) as to the best course of action. Ray thought they should not move on, but Aaron said this was because of the girl from the youth hostel. Ray, furious, hit him. So it was decided: they would walk down to Seatoller, then up the neighbouring valley, past Sourmilk Gill, the route they had planned last night. Langdale would be far more hospitable in this weather than Honister, Aaron informed them; there were two pubs, a shop at Elterwater, even a bus sometimes to Ambleside. Tim had told him this on the journey up.

Aaron and John wore shorts. If they were going to get wet there was no point in soaking their jeans right through, they said. Tim walked behind his beloved, staring at his legs, at the blond hair wet and plastered to the skin. Tendon, muscle; bend forward, straighten: the same action thousands and thousands of times. As easy as breathing; what motor inside made such complexity function perfectly, without the need to think? The rain increased. Tim could not remember when he was last so drenched. Jeans, socks, boots had become part of his flesh; the water seemed to act like glue. Rain dripped from hair and eyelashes, noses and chins. Conversation was minimal, less frequent than their nostrils sniffling, just Ray's repetitive lament that they should have stopped at Honister.

John, shouldering the burden of the tent, and because the way was steeply uphill, said wearily 'Why don't you just fuck off, Franco?' and after that there was silence.

They rested near Sprinkling Tarn. Tim, looking at the three hunched figures, thought they were as much a part of the landscape as the stones, the mud, the sheet of water; patient and sodden, enduring the weight of the weather, life shrunk down inside them. Colours were brilliant, green grass and copper fern like wet paint on a canvas just finished. A few yards off, all round them the grey fog, a tent of fog, as if the whole world was wrapped in this thick impenetrable wool, and the small circle of ground they could see was the only life left on earth.

Near Esk Hause, Ray said 'I've lost the compass.'

They stopped, searched, and told him he was a cretin. They could not find it. 'Where did you lose it? Exactly?' Aaron asked.

'I don't know. I realised just now I no longer had it.'

'When did you last look at it?'

'Sprinkling Tarn, I think.'

They glared at him, annoyed. 'You can take the tent, Franco,' John said, and dropped it on the ground. Ray picked it up, humbly.

'I don't think it matters at the moment,' Tim ventured. 'We're on the motorway. Scafell Pike, last exit, just here. End of motorway, Langdale, three miles. The service station.'

'It's well marked,' Aaron agreed. 'We can't go wrong. Come on.'

They continued uphill. 'Tomorrow, Ray, you can buy a compass,' John said.

'I will, boss.'

Half an hour later Tim was worried. Angle Tarn should have been reached; they should have been going downhill before now, but the way was undulating, little ups and downs; it was no wider than a sheep track. He stopped and looked about him, frowning.

'What's the matter?' Aaron asked.

'I don't think this is right. And I can't tell whether we've strayed off to the north or south of the track. North, I think. The other side's all crags, Hanging Knotts, Bowfell.'

Aaron stared in disbelief. 'You mean we're lost?'

'I don't know.'

They walked on. The path disappeared totally and they were stumbling over boulders and clumps of heather. 'But there's your tarn,' Ray said.

It was too small, not much more than a very big puddle. Despite the rain it looked as if it had once been larger; reeds, a sinister dark green all round the edges, rustled. 'It's not,' Tim said. 'Angle's the size of Sprinkling. I don't know what that is.'

'What are we going to do?'

They pored over the map, as if the secret would be there, but none of them had any inspiration.

Aaron was angry. 'It's all your fault!'

Ray looked so miserable that John said mildly 'Anyone could lose a compass.'

They walked a little way in each direction, but there always seemed to be some insuperable difficulty, crags or marsh, or a sheer drop into a void of fog. They tried to retrace their steps to Esk Hause but even the sheep track had vanished. They found themselves again by the tarn. John, Ray and Aaron looked at Tim for help; Tim was the only one, after all, who knew the mountains. But in this hour of glory (Aaron wanting assistance from him was an honour he had never imagined he would achieve) he knew he would fail. He studied the map for clues, concentrating ferociously. 'This could be High Hause Tarn,' he said. 'We're probably on Glaramara.'

'Glaramara!' Aaron exclaimed. 'Never heard of it.'

'Well, it's a nice name,' John said.

Tim looked round wildly, as if the answer might be written on the stones, in the mud, or whispered by the reeds. 'There's only one possible thing we can do,' he said, trying to sound full of confidence. 'Camp here and stay put till the cloud lifts. We can dry out and eat. There's water from the tarn for cooking. Stay here tonight.' He looked at his watch. 'Four o'clock. Yes, stay here, and tomorrow we'll be able to see where we are; the fog can't last for ever.'

They obeyed him without question, relieved to be doing something normal, glad to accept authority. These three meekly doing what he, Tim Keegan, told them: the sensation of pleasure was very sweet.

The inside of the tent was like a damp airing cupboard. Wet clothes wrung out and steaming, dangling so that they muffled faces like a clammy cold bat when a body shifted unexpectedly; bare limbs and torsos, not always possible in the little space to say whose was which: Ray, hairy and thick-set but surprisingly neat in his movements, Aaron sprawled on his front on a sleeping-bag, sleek as a well-groomed cat, red knickers his only adornment, John, white-skinned but with stronger muscles than either of them. Tim struggled heroically near the tent flaps with the primus and a pan full of sausages, battling to ward off the rain and drive out the cooking fumes, hoping his efforts diverted attention from his own thin legs and arms.

After the meal, it was pop on the transistor, Ray and John moving chess-pieces on a travelling set, Tim with Blake, and Aaron with *Confessions*. They all inspected Tim's book of poetry and it passed without comment.

'Don't let it drive you to playing with yourself,' John said, nodding at Aaron's paperback.

'Blake would more likely do that.' What did he mean, Tim wondered, but he did not ask.

'I've been blind for years,' Ray said, and they all laughed, even Tim.

You never know what is enough unless you know what is more than enough. Oh, for the chance!

How can the bird that is born for joy
Sit in the cage and sing?

'It interests me, that's all.' Aaron had asked why he'd brought school work with him.

'I can't get on with poetry. Not that stuff anyway. It's like untying string.'

'That's good,' Tim said, after a moment's thought.

'What is?'

'What you said. Untying string. Yes, it's very much like that.'

'I wish I'd brought my guitar.'

'I've heard you. You're good.'

'Where?'

'At school once; you were playing it all one lunch hour.'

'I didn't know you were listening. Well . . . I'm trying to start up a group. Aaron's Rod, I'm calling it.'

'D. H. Lawrence?'

'Eh? It's a flower.'

28

'Yes. Is that what you want to do, when you leave school? Confessions of Aaron, pop star.'

'Me? I don't know. I haven't really thought about it.' He was silent, then asked 'What about you?'

'University. I hope.'

'You're a queer one, Tim.'

Something in the voice told him it was deliberate, a challenge. Did he dare pick up such a gauntlet? His heart suddenly started to flutter, and his stomach heaved. 'Am I?' he croaked. Aaron nodded. Tim picked it up, the very first time since he knew that he was. 'Does it show?'

'Not really.'

Relief. 'Does it matter?'

'Who to?'

'You.'

Aaron was puzzled. 'Why should it bother me? It bothers you, I guess.'

'Maybe it does.' The understatement of the century. 'You . . . aren't.'

He looked amused. 'What do you think, big sister?' He turned over, away from Tim, concentrating on *Confessions*. Tim was trembling.

'Good morning, world!' Tim, wrapped only in a patch-work quilt, stood at the slit window that looked down the estuary, and greeted a section of the New Model which could be seen, encamped, in the distance.

'Come away from there.' Anthony was still in bed. 'A naked man! They are, after all, Puritans.'

'They're about a mile away, towards Countess Wear. Having breakfast I should think. Sir Hardress Waller's merry men! It's daringly close, though, isn't it?'

'They know how weak we are.' Anthony yawned. 'I

29

ought to be up, but I have no relish for it. Brew me a hot drink, Tim, and cut me off a slice of cold beef.'

A deafening explosion, close to, made them jump with fright. Tim dropped to the floor, below window level. 'What is it?' he whispered. Several more explosions, equally loud, followed.

'Idiot. It's *our* ordnance. See what they're firing at, will you?'

But Tim moved to the other window, attracted by the sound of horses' hooves on the cobbles. South Street, from end to end, was filled with armed men on horseback. Anthony threw back the bed-covers and dressed hurriedly. 'Put your clothes on,' he ordered. 'And stay in this room, out of sight. I do not want people to know you're in here.' He ran to the door.

'Why? I was assigned to you, wasn't I?'

'I can do without trouble.'

'But . . . am I not supposed to be here?'

'I'll explain at another time.' He rushed downstairs. Tim listened. There was a short, heated argument; the commander of the horse was apparently not pleased at being kept waiting. The gate should have been opened five minutes previously. Anthony apologised, and moments later the throng of cavalry was surging forwards, out of the city. The gate was shut again, but Anthony did not return. He came up the stairs, then continued on to the muniment room. There seemed to be several people with him. Distributing arms to the citizens, Tim thought; this was the start of it, and his guess was proved right when he saw a group of men walking briskly up the street, carrying muskets. More people could be heard tramping up the staircase, and, after a while, Anthony shouted crossly for Tim to hurry up with the breakfast. Tim, dressed by now, scuttled round, preparing food. Should he risk Anthony's anger by taking it upstairs, after being told not to leave the living-quarters? He hovered, undecided.

'Tim! Where's that meal? Bring it here!'

He put the plates on a tray and rushed up to the muniment room. Anthony was checking stores. 'Don't mind my temper,' he said. 'Everything has to work to a precise pattern. Just do as you're told and ignore me shouting. Does it upset you?'

'No. I think I like being needed.'

'Good.' He looked at Tim, quite friendly now. 'Go down and make the room spotless.'

Was Anthony a secret sympathizer of the Parliament, he wondered, as he made the bed. He remembered the hint of disappointment in his eyes, that first time they had met. And the strange remark just now about doing without trouble. Royalist Exeter was terrified of a Parliament victory. Stories were whispered by one man to another of the atrocities committed by the New Model. The Puritans were monsters, scarcely human, guilty of deeds so shameful and revolting that tongue dared not even name them. Should they gain control of the city the best one could hope for would be the merciful release of a quick death. Such tales, Tim knew, were nonsense, had no foundation on even the slimmest of truths. The men of the Parliament were men no different from the King's: two eyes, two arms, two legs, with as much diversity of thought and feeling as any group of human beings, the same selfish or unselfish passions. They would not slaughter for a cause. They simply wanted the right to exist in their own particular way, unpersecuted by Royalist authority, in peace and as equals. Anthony, Tim felt, might be one of them, and at the appropriate time he would declare himself.

While he swept and dusted and tidied, the cannons fired sporadically. It was something less than a major assault on the Roundhead forces, more like a token gesture. Tim, looking out of the window every so often, could see that the balls fell short of Sir Hardress's lines and did no damage. It was the growl of a dying animal, not an attack to kill.

Anthony left at dinner-time and did not return till early evening. Tim, alone all afternoon, had nothing to occupy himself with except gaze at the view. He was not bored, for towards three o'clock something like a real skirmish began to develop and he could observe it all from where he stood. Sir Hardress's cavalry had advanced from their forward positions of the previous night, and as they were crossing a stream a quarter of a mile to the south of the gatehouse, they were set upon by the troops who had ridden out from the city that morning. It was too far away to observe in detail, but the noise of firing was real enough, as was the clash of steel, the terror of the horses, and the cries of men, wounded or dying, falling to the ground. The King's soldiers attacked with a bravado that was at times plain stupid, or maybe it was born of an intense hatred for the other side; the Puritans behaved with coolness, patience and greater military discipline. Nevertheless they would have been severely defeated in the long run had not an attachment of foot come to their support, and the Royalist horse, driven off at last, were made to flee to the safety of the city as best they might, ragged, bleeding, dejected. Some prisoners, Tim noticed, were taken by Sir Hardress's troops, but these were not killed or harmed in any way that he could see. The Puritans attended to their own dead and injured, and eventually retreated behind their fortifications at Countess Wear.

32

Jake, the sexton, walked along the wall. Tim left his place by the window and went outside to talk to him.

'Destroying their energies, both parties,' Jake said, jerking his thumb in the direction of the approaching cavalry. 'Why don't they find something better to do?'

'You never thought of fighting, then?' Tim asked.

'Me? With a wife and two young girls to feed?'

'You're married?' He was surprised; Jake seemed so young, not more than twenty or twenty-two at most. His face was almost an innocent little boy's face.

'Why shouldn't I be?'

'No reason.'

'Don't you find yourself caught too early like I did. One hour's fun and you're lumbered for life. Repent at leisure.'

'It won't happen to me.'

Jake looked him up and down. 'No, I don't imagine it will,' he said, and turned away to unlock the door of Holy Trinity tower. He knows, Tim thought. Does he mind? Jake went into the church and the door slammed after him, leaving Tim staring.

Over dinner Anthony said 'You are a Parliament man, Tim.'

Deciding that they knew one another sufficiently now to admit, he said 'Yes,' but nevertheless with a beating heart.

'A man must be whatever he is,' Anthony said, philosophically. 'Regardless of the odds.'

'So are you, I think.'

'Me?' The astonishment was genuine. 'Whatever made you say that?'

'I thought . . . I had guessed.'

He looked at Tim coldly, but before either of them could speak there was a knock at the door. It was Saint-Hill. Anthony did not offer him a chair, but, undaunted, he seated himself and began to talk. It looked as though he would stay a long time. Exeter, he said, was in no fit shape to hold out against the enemy; it was even less well provided for than in the siege of 1643. There were no supplies in the shops; hoarding of food was minimal, and the likelihood of men breaking out of the city to obtain fresh meat and vegetables was remote. The populace would not starve at once, but hardship before long would be severe. And despite this, the authorities were growing more arbitrary and dictatorial; only this afternoon there had been a number of families dragged from their homes and taken to gaol for no crime at all other than being suspected of Parliament sympathy, women, children and tiny babies included. They had all come from the parish of St. Olave; it was rumoured that tomorrow similar arrests would occur in St. Mary Arches, and would continue, daily, parish by parish, until non-Conformity was entirely locked up.

Tim listened with much more sympathy than on the previous occasion. True, the voice was like that of a bishop in a pulpit—it spoke not to Anthony or Tim; it just spoke—but the words made more sense than last time.

'Will you open the gate and let me out?' Saint-Hill asked.

'What for?'

'I propose to walk to the Roundhead lines and seek an interview with my Lord Fairfax. I shall tell him how to enter the city without the necessity of a siege.'

'You're mad.'

Saint-Hill nodded. 'Yes, the world would think so, certainly.'

'And what of your Royalist principles?'

'In no way shaken. The restoration of all the King's rights and honours is what is worth fighting for; the sub-

34

ordination of the Commons to its proper place in the scheme of things is what God Almighty cries out for. But I will not see this city and its innocent inhabitants destroyed in that conflict.'

'Your logic is somewhat cloudy,' Anthony said, sarcastically. 'You serve the King, yet would surrender one of his last remaining strongholds in the West.'

Tim accompanied them downstairs. Anthony opened the gate a fraction and Saint-Hill left. The night, chilly with a restless little wind moaning and a hint of rain, soon swallowed him up, though his footsteps in the dusty road could be heard for some moments afterwards.

'The enemy will have a surprise before they sleep,' Anthony said. 'A man so convinced of his own rightness that he thinks he can, by himself, alter history inevitably goes to a quick destruction.'

'What will Fairfax do?'

'Assuming Saint-Hill is granted an interview, which I imagine is highly unlikely, I think the lord general will laugh.'

Tim, worried, wanted to check all the equipment; the weather was deteriorating all the time. The rain had increased and a strong wind was blowing. They could be marooned here for days. Fortunately the tent was excellent, brand new and waterproof, except near the flaps, which had been open when he was cooking. Rain had also gusted in when one or other of them had gone out during the evening to pee, but, all things considered, wet was so far not a problem. The enclosed space would be more of a difficulty if they had to stay here all day tomorrow; it was now intimate and friendly, but it would soon cause tempers to flare.

He could hardly ask the other three for an inventory of

their belongings. He tried to recall what he had noticed in their rucksacks. All four had proper footwear—good mountain-walking boots—and thick socks, sensible anoraks, and sufficient dry clothing for one complete change. Shorts were a good idea for rain, and he wished he'd thought of it himself, particularly as the weather was not cold. No-one was likely to suffer from hypothermia. The sleeping-bags were adequate, so was the cooking equipment. Food was the main worry.

John and Ray were discussing Ipswich Town's performance last week. Aaron, Tim noticed, was watching him; presumably wondering why his eyes darted, checking, from one thing to another. 'What food do you have left?' he asked.

Aaron fished around in his rucksack. 'Kendal mint-cake. Apples, four. Packet of Sainsbury's ginger cream biscuits. Why?'

'We're running out.'

'We buy more in Langdale tomorrow. That's what we decided.'

'If . . .' Aaron looked startled as he realized. 'Don't say anything. What do they have?'

'I don't know. Ray's got a few oranges, and the cheese sandwiches he didn't eat on the train. John has some raisins. And an unopened packet of Number Six.'

'Hmm. I've got two bars of chocolate. And tomorrow's breakfast; four eggs, bacon, and the rest of the bread.'

Aaron thought for a moment, said nothing, then returned to his book. Ray was recounting the details of his last trip to Portman Road where Ipswich Town had beaten Derby County four nil. His tale was like the recital of a battle: attack, charge, assault, retreat. John, losing interest, said 'At least they say Portman Road has the prettiest girls. In the spectators, I mean.' He sniggered.

'Ramón,' Aaron called, 'what would you do if Ipswich were home to Réal Madrid? Ramón Manuel Suñer Azaña? Boyo.'

'Don't know. Very difficult decision.'

'Go on. Who would you support?' Ray was silent, knowing he was being provoked. 'Fran-co! Fran-co! Fran-co!'

'If I was a German'—he was trying to be sweet reasonableness—'would you call me Hitler?'

'Yes!'

'And if you were Argentine we'd call you Evita,' John said.

'Get lost, Suffolk peasant!'

'Per-ón! Per-ón! Per-ón!' Aaron chanted. 'Don't cry for me, Ar-h-entina!'

'Stop it,' Tim said, quietly.

Aaron turned to him disdainfully, and said 'Bummer.'

'We might be in here for days!' His voice rose, and he hoped his blush wasn't visible. 'Do you want it to be a battleground?'

Silence. John looked surprised. Ray, evidently, had not taken it in, for he said 'My great-uncle was executed by the Fascists. My grandfather destroyed two tanks single-handed. There were twenty thousand people living on the pavements of Madrid, and when the city was on fire from the air-raids you could hear them: "¡No pas-ar-án! ¡No pas-ar-án!" When Bilbao was captured, the Germans inspected all the factories and, because they were undamaged, production was speeded up to make more guns for the rebels, *and* for Hitler. And you wonder why I don't like being called Franco!'

'Only a joke,' John said. 'A silly one, I daresay.'

'How did they escape?' Tim asked. 'Your family?'

'Grandad was with the Republican army all the war.

Málaga, Guadalajara, Teruel. When Barcelona fell, he and Grandma . . . gave up, I suppose. They walked to France, over the freezing Pyrenees. My dad was three; his fourth birthday was the day they crossed the frontier.'

'Where are they now?'

'My grandparents? They live with us. Grandad worked in the docks until he retired last year. My dad's on the car ferries, head chef. We all live in the one flat.'

'Have you ever been to Spain?'

'*Been to Spain?* My God, until last year we'd have all been shot as soon as we set foot in the country!'

'He's been to Spain every day of his life,' Aaron said. 'In his mind.'

'That's true enough,' Ray admitted. 'Yes, I'd like to go back there.'

'Go *back?* You can't go back to somewhere you've never been!'

Ray grinned. 'We fight all the old battles in our kitchen. Brunete's Grandad's speciality. I've seen him do that, yes, many times; hardly a word changes each performance. He lines up the kitchen cups; they're Franco's mob, and the whisky tumblers are our battalions. To show the difference in class, he says. He's good at imitating the politicians, Companys in particular. Oh, but you wouldn't know who Companys was. ¡*Visca la Llibertat!* He was shot.'

'I've heard it all,' Aaron said. 'Too often.'

'Ron, they can't help it! They were *there!*'

'They could leave you out of it. You're English, a Suffolk ploughboy! Do you know'—Aaron turned to Tim—'if he went out with a Catholic girl they'd cut him off with a shilling!'

'Why?'

'Because the Church was on the rebels' side,' Ray

38

explained. 'That creeping Jesus, the Pope, supported Franco throughout, even though the Basques were Catholic to a man, no stauncher Catholics in the world, and Republican to a man. My family hates Catholics. Grandad was an Anarchist, you see.'

'What's the point of fighting about it now?' Aaron said. 'It's all history. And very boring for everybody else.'

'Ron, they can't *help* it!'

'*You* can. You can stand up for being you, can't you?'

Ray looked perplexed. 'What do you mean?'

'I don't know.' Aaron turned over, searching for the place he'd lost in his book. 'I don't have these problems. My dad runs a pub and he's soft as a mashed turnip, lets me do almost anything I like. Mum's an old nag. I don't take any notice and neither do my brothers. Yes, I've got grandparents, too; they live a stone's throw from us and Grandma's a bit sharp. But I wouldn't let anybody interfere with my life, not the way you do.'

'Depends what you're born to,' Tim said.

'What are yours like, then?' John asked.

He was about to reply, but remembering what Ray had said about Catholics, he decided it was not really the moment. 'They're all right,' he said, looking in his rucksack for Blake. And, after a moment, John reopened the subject of Ipswich Town with Ray.

All right! How did you tell a mother who was Irish and devoutly Catholic that you knew you were homosexual? There would be an instant drama: 'Are you trying to kill me?' and she would pack him off to Father Sullivan to be sorted out. There were no possible ways the two could be reconciled. Being homosexual, the priest would say, is not a sin in itself, though it was certainly not a condition to be desired. It was a severe handicap, perhaps a mental illness,

and a homosexual act—in thought, word, or deed—was a
mortal sin. Pope Paul had spoken on this matter not long
ago, reaffirming what the Church had taught throughout
the ages: sexual behaviour in human beings was only
acceptable to God within marriage; its purpose was for the
procreation of children. Pleasure, fulfillment, happiness:
non-starters.

Tim found this hard. To be forbidden, for the rest of his
life, to touch, stroke, kiss, let alone adventure further with
any person of his own sex made a mockery of being given
the blessing of existence in the first place. At the same time
he could not reject the Church, the faith of his fathers, two
thousand years of authority. Until recently it had been
positively painful to hear Catholicism criticized: two terms
back they had started Chaucer, and he'd been shocked by
the ironic sneers at worldly nuns and lecherous friars. His
English teacher had become quite impatient with his
attitude. But somehow, in some way, in the distant future
—or maybe not so far off perhaps—he would have to
choose. 'To be adult is to have the power to choose,' he
remembered the Headmaster saying in one of their sixth-
form World Affairs periods.

Blake would have agreed. Expect poison from standing
water. He who desires but acts not, breeds pestilence.
Inside myself, inside myself.

Extraordinary the hold parents had. It was the guilt they
could induce; the all-we've-sacrificed-to-give-you syndrome. Even though he had been in conflict with both of
them for some while now, slowly examining their standards,
slowly rejecting them. His mother's snobbery: table napkins
instead of serviettes; 'shut up!' was a rude expression;
wearing a school cap every morning as he left home (she
insisted), to remove it of course as soon as he was round the

corner. If he said—and naturally he never would—words like semen or vagina she would die on the spot. How had he arrived in this world? Shut your eyes and think of England? (Ireland.) Since he was born they had slept in separate beds; they were thirty-two at the time. The pressure on him to work, work, work! Education, the last and greatest of panaceas! Just to fulfill what she had always wanted for herself and never achieved!

Dad, whose mode of speech was the imperative mood: instructions, negatives. There's a right way and a wrong way of doing everything. Fold your flannel in four when you wash. Tuck your shirt inside your pants. (Knickers! Tim would scream, inside his head.) You can't learn to drive the car yet; you're too young. I'm seventeen, Dad. I don't care how old you are, you're . . . what's the use? Give in, creep by, bent reed in the storm. Oh we don't want to watch that sort of thing! Switch it off! Bruce Forsyth, Are you being Served, Porridge, Top of the Pops, etcetera, etcetera. And why don't you play games like any decent lad? When I was at school I was captain of the fourth eleven. And get a haircut. Clean yourself up (euphemism for shave). Be a nice neat replica of boring humourless unhappy old me with my twenty-seven years' secure job in the civil service.

If only there had been a brother or a sister!

At least the idea of this trip had been allowed, welcomed even. 'Do you good to get out in the open air, lads of your own age.'

How lucky to be Aaron! Fancying girls, Dad soft as a mashed turnip, brothers (there were three, David, Martin and Peter), able to do more or less exactly what he liked. The body so sleek, slim, desirable, and, Tim guessed, as soon as he'd discovered sex he'd been having it, not a trace of guilt or shame. How extraordinary that people were so different!

> Some are Born to sweet delight,
> Some are Born to Endless Night.

He lay awake long after the others slept. The wind blew fiercely and the tent strained, its canvas banging and flapping. But it held firm. Maybe the low cloud would have disappeared by morning, and they could walk easily enough to Langdale.

Aaron, breathing evenly. Tim stretched out a hand and touched his face.

He was the first to open his eyes. No wind, just steady rain soaking into the saturated earth. He peered out. Dense grey cloud, worse than yesterday. He slipped back inside his warm sleeping-bag.

CHAPTER THREE

It soon appeared probable that the Parliament army was in no hurry to begin a frontal assault on Exeter. Observation from the walls, confirmed by reports from spies that filtered through to the citizens, showed that the New Model was more concerned with digging itself in, tending its sick and wounded, and finding suitable winter quarters, than with launching a grand attack. Rumours abounded. So many different stories, often flatly contradictory, circulated, that Anthony said the city was as leaky as a sieve. When Tim asked what he meant, he said that, despite the closure of the gates, the number of possible ways out was so numerous that, under the cover of darkness, people fled through the fields to the Puritan lines. Mostly they were cowards wishing to escape from the hardships of a long siege and the reprisals they feared would occur when Exeter finally capitulated, but some were employed to obtain first-hand information about the movements and plans of the enemy and report back to the authorities. This latter was undoubtedly a two-way traffic; a stranger noticed at dusk in the city streets could well be a Roundhead intelligence man. In a civil war it was not at all easy to tell friend from foe; speech, gesture, clothes could be identical on either side.

Rumour had it that the Governor, Sir John Berkeley, was already in communication with Fairfax concerning the terms of the surrender. Rumour had it that he had refused Fairfax's proposals outright. Then, rumour, deciding that perhaps too much credence had been given to Berkeley's defiance, let it be whispered that ten commissioners from both parties were in secret session at Poltimore, the home of Sir John Bampfylde, some three miles north-east of the city. Negotiations were extremely delicate, rumour said; Parliament's biggest prize in Exeter would undoubtedly be the Princess Henrietta Maria, the King's infant daughter, who had lived at Bedford House since her birth there four years previously. The Queen, of course, had long since fled to France, but on no account could Sir John Berkeley allow the little princess to fall into the hands of the Puritans. Time, however, was on Fairfax's side; he could pitch his demands fairly high (not so high that history would deem him unreasonable or tyrannical) but high enough for Parliament to be satisfied, and know that he only had to wait patiently and Berkeley would capitulate. And, rumour added, there were other reasons for lack of haste; his army needed a pause after their long march into the West Country, for his men had been weakened by epidemics of fever.

Speculation was rife, too, concerning the fate of the thousand Royalist cavalry under the command of Lord George Goring, who had disappeared from Exeter the night before Fairfax had completed his encirclement. Some said they had regrouped at Okehampton, and, refreshed now, were advancing to relieve the city and chase the New Model out of Devon. No, they had been surprised by Cromwell's men advancing from Bow and had been cut to pieces. Nonsense, Cromwell was still at Crediton, observing from a distance; Fairfax wanted the capital of the South-West to fall into his own hands. In that case the Royalist army had gone to the aid of the besiegers at Plymouth. Or, knowing that the cause was hopeless, perhaps they had dispersed quietly to safe places in the countryside.

Only one piece of information was certain. Powderham Castle, the last remaining outpost in Royalist hands, fell to the enemy. The castle, standing on the western side of the estuary, was stormed by a handful of Sir Hardress Waller's men, led by Colonel Hammond. They had crossed the river during the night. This piece of news was received in Exeter with profound gloom.

Daily the remnant of the Royalist horse left the city, more to boost morale and show the populace that the war was still being vigorously prosecuted than for any positive military reasons. They achieved a few mild successes, picking off a Parliament straggler here and there, raiding the odd farm for supplies. Their own losses, however, hardly made even this policy worthwhile, and rumour had it that Berkeley, whose control over his military commanders was imperfect, was incensed at the difficulties it was causing to his deliberations at Poltimore.

Tim watched these clashes from the gatehouse window, but otherwise he was bored by the inactivity that preparations for a siege induced. Anthony was increasingly occupied with various affairs about which he said little and which took up a great deal of his time (the illegal distribution of food, Tim guessed; the supplies upstairs had dropped considerably, and there were frequent sounds of footsteps and murmured conversations from the storeroom). Tim spent much of the days now away from the gatehouse, exploring the city, though he always made sure

45

he served meals on time. Lack of punctuality about meals invariably made Anthony fly into a rage.

The city was like standing water, stagnant. There were very few people in the streets, for there was almost nothing to buy in the shops or at the markets. Those who were abroad often appeared to walk in an aimless fashion as if their only purpose was to exercise. Every third person, it was said, was a spy, either for the Royalist administration or else in the pay of Parliament. Neighbours who had lived contentedly now stared at their acquaintances with looks of dark suspicion. The favourite place for a stroll was the city walls, where people hoped to relieve the tedium with a glimpse of horsemen fighting; this sometimes caused annoyance to the soldiers on duty who thought such activities hampered their stint of observation, and more than one fist fight was the result.

There was no wheeled traffic of any sort, and grass began to grow in the cobbles, even in the High Street. Offensive smells increased; there was no means of removing excrement, not even to the river, which lay tantalisingly out of reach beyond the west gate. Drinking water was scarce; the authorities considered how it might be rationed, but no plan was put into operation. Disease was a threat, particularly in the poorer parishes of St Mary Major, St George, and St Mary Steps. Churches were full: the Sunday services—celebrated everywhere in a manner to which Archbishop Laud would have given total approval—became the chief events of the social calendar, were attended, indeed looked forward to, even by those who normally skimped or evaded. The Dissenting places of worship, on the other hand, were padlocked; some had been mysteriously destroyed by fire.

One afternoon, when Tim was wandering without much

purpose near the Guildhall he saw a troop of horse clattering towards him on the cobbles. He paid little attention, but he was jolted abruptly from his thoughts by a strident voice shouting at him. 'You! Who are you, and what are you doing?'

He looked up at the cavalry captain, a fierce red-faced giant with enormous grey whiskers. A dozen men had reined in their horses.

'I'm Tim Keegan. The servant to the warder of the south gate.'

'What are you about here, so far from your duties?'

'There's . . . little to do this afternoon.'

'You're a fit, able-bodied man?'

'Yes, sir.'

'Hmmm. I have a sick recruit.' He turned, and bawled at the rearmost soldier: 'Evans! Get off that damned horse and return to barracks. Give this man your cutlass and musket. And your pistol.'

'But . . .' Tim quavered.

'But what?' The captain leaned down and glared ferociously. He did not seem to be the sort of person one argued with.

'Nothing, sir.'

'Good. Just as well for you. Now get up on that blasted horse and stop wasting my time.'

So Tim found himself riding out through the east gate into the parish of St Sidwell. The houses here lay all in ruins; they had been blown up by Goring's men in order to avoid giving shelter to the advancing columns of Fairfax's army. The inhabitants had been forced to find refuge inside the city walls, and most of them, who had once been of the Royalist persuasion, had been turned by this piece of unnecessary destruction (as they saw it) into Parliament

47

sympathizers. Only the church survived, though this had lost its roof and all its windows. The tower, nevertheless, offered the Roundheads an excellent position from which they could fire into the city itself, and the fact of its still standing unharmed seemed to underline the thoughtless nature of the Cavaliers' action.

At the parish end the expedition turned south-east towards Heavitree. In the dip below the village they were shot at by some inaccurate Parliament marksmen hidden in a copse, so, digging in their spurs, they turned tail and dashed across the fields in the direction of Whipton. This village, the nearest to Exeter in Puritan hands, they skirted carefully. The Roundheads made no sign of having seen them, though the presence of the King's men must have been quite obvious. The captain gave an order to halt in a secluded lane from which the low white outline of Poltimore House could be observed in the distance. Tim, at the rear, gazed about at the countryside. It was a peaceful autumn afternoon of hazy sunshine. Trees were a riot of gold, copper and red; beechnuts lay on the ground; thistledown and columns of gnats floated in the air. The fields were deserted, no cows nor sheep, no labourers at their seasonal tasks, and everywhere he looked there were signs that the rhythm of the year had been interrupted by war: a haystack, half-built and now rotting, a field of barley left half-reaped, unkempt overgrown hedges, ditches full to the brim with decaying leaves.

The captain gave the order to move, then driving his horse from a canter into a gallop, and brandishing his sword, yelled 'Charge!' The speed was hair-raising, and Tim, covered in dust and mud from the animals in front, felt certain he must fall off and break his neck. Gradually, try as he might to keep up, the rest of the cavalry drew

48

away, and eventually, having lost them, he reined in his horse under a tree on some high ground. From here he watched them follow a road that discreetly avoided both Whipton and Heavitree, and soon all they were was a cloud of dust rushing towards the river, where, he guessed, they intended to water their steeds. The whole excursion had had no point whatsoever, except to give exercise to rider and horse, and perhaps to show to the Roundheads that there was still some life in the Cavaliers.

A twig snapping nearby instantly made him fearful, and he looked to his musket. Was there some Parliamentary sniper hidden in the trees? To be killed by the men towards whom his natural sympathies inclined would be lunatic. There *was* someone there. The day was windless, yet the bushes shook slightly. He raised the gun. Then lowered it, for into the clearing staggered a figure he recognized, torn and blood-stained though the clothes were and wild the face and hair. It was Saint-Hill.

Saint-Hill was delighted beyond measure to see Tim, and in his customary manner of accepting what had not quite been offered, he made to climb up on the horse. They trotted slowly back to the city. Saint-Hill's mission had, apparently, not been a success, but only he seemed surprised. He had not at first been allowed to see Fairfax, but had been interrogated, at length and arrogantly, by an underling. Then he was blindfolded and made to walk a great distance, eventually finding himself inside a house. When he was allowed to see, he was in a room in the middle of which was a long table, six men seated on either side. At the head of the table sat Sir Thomas Fairfax, at the foot Sir John Berkeley. It was the dining-room of Poltimore.

'I was made to repeat my story,' he said. 'And when I

stumbled, as I was bound to do, six Royalist commanders and the Governor being present, I was prodded, most uncomfortably, by a sword. Sir John was enraged, and demanded I should be taken out instantly and shot. Sir Thomas, an urbane and ironic man, did not agree. He assured the Governor, on his word of honour as a gentleman, that he would not, in any circumstances, have acted on my suggestions. It was quite contrary to the rules of war. I must be an imbecile, he said, harmless no doubt, but obviously deranged. A good whipping was all I needed.'

'And were you whipped?'

'Yes.'

'Are you in pain?'

'Less than I was. But my back is a mass of raw flesh.'

It was not maybe the fate Saint-Hill's idea merited, Tim thought, but the man, considering his foolhardiness, was lucky to be alive. Belief in oneself and nothing else, it occurred to him, was poor clothing with which to face the wily ways of the world. 'How did you escape?' he asked.

'I didn't have to escape. They turned me loose into the night, covered in blood as I was. As I left I heard from the dining-room the noise of clinking glass and loud laughter.'

'Some interesting little deal is being hatched in there, I suppose.'

'Yes. A considerable sum of money will probably change hands. Berkeley and his advisers will be allowed to leave the city unharmed; liberal and fine-sounding guarantees concerning the fate of Princess Henrietta Maria will be announced together with proclamations on the sanctity of property and the freedom of religious worship for all denominations. Berkeley will surrender; Fairfax march in (he will claim that he captured Exeter without a shot being

50

fired), then the Puritan soldiers will have free rein to sack and pillage as much as they like.'

'I had always heard that Fairfax was a decent, humane man, that the New Model had an iron discipline.'

'I've heard otherwise.'

There was a long silence. It was good to be alive, Tim thought; the ride had refreshed him, given him a sense of well-being: the sour smells of autumn, the weak sunlight turning the distant hills gold, the estuary glittering towards the sea. And there was work to do now, real work, not insignificant little jobs that Anthony could easily do himself if he had a mind to. Tim had Saint-Hill, had to wash his wounds, nurse him, restore him to health. He was needed.

'We'll go in by the south gate,' he said. 'It will be safer.'

'I must shelter. There would be danger in my own house.'

Anthony let them through without comment, but as soon as Saint-Hill had dismounted, a dozen soldiers emerged from behind the church and arrested him. They attempted to drag Tim off as well, but released him when Anthony intervened.

Tim was appalled, but common sense stopped him from protesting aloud at what the soldiers were doing. 'What will happen to him?' he asked, despairingly.

Anthony gestured across his throat, and a strangled gasp came from his mouth. 'You are lucky not to suffer in the same way!' he shouted, and this was the first sentence of an angry tirade, in which he berated Tim at length for his thoughtlessness and stupidity.

'I couldn't leave him . . . what else could I do? . . . I had no option!'

'If you survive long enough, which I doubt, maybe you'll learn to ignore the requests of men like Saint-Hill. It nearly clapped you in gaol! And as for him, he'll be dead by tomorrow morning. If you'd left him alone to wander round the countryside, maybe he would have lived!'

Sleep would not return, so he studied the map. The names were fascinating—The Lord's Rake, Crinkle Crags, Gavel Neese, Pike of Blisco, Aaron Slack, Pike of Stickle. Not one Sourmilk Gill, but several. He was fairly certain they were by High Hause Tarn on Glaramara, but which was the right direction? He had an obscure conviction that north lay on the far side of the tarn, but there was no possible way of discovering for certain. John stirred, crawled from his sleeping-bag and went out to pee.

'We should have brought another compass,' Tim said, when he returned.

John, equally dismayed by the weather, said, shortly, 'Well, we didn't.'

'Quite mad to bring only one.'

After a while John asked 'What are we going to do?'

'I don't know. Which direction do you think is north?'

He scratched his head. 'I'd say, a wild guess, beyond the tarn.'

'I've that feeling too.'

Breakfast was eaten in gloomy silence. Aaron grumbled that he was still hungry, and took the Kendal mint-cake out of his rucksack.

'Don't eat that!' Tim warned.

'Why not? And who the hell do you think you are telling me what to do?'

'We don't know when we're going to get our next meal.'

This truth was so obvious that Aaron replaced it. 'Wish I'd never come,' he said. 'Half-term bloody Monday. I could be lying in bed at home.' No-one answered.

'Do we move or do we stop here?' Ray asked, eventually. Again, silence, and he said 'Tim, I'm talking to you!'

'Stay. For the time being. No point in getting drenched. And walking round in circles, maybe. If the rain stops well . . .'

'Which direction?'

'Any way that's down. Borrowdale, Langdale, Eskdale even; it doesn't matter so long as we reach civilization.'

'Civilization!' Aaron snorted. 'Whose idea was this crummy expedition in the first place? Back home we'd be playing records and thinking about where we'd go out this evening.' He opened the tent flaps. 'I'm not staying in here a moment longer,' he said, and went outside.

'Where are you going?' John asked.

'To find the way down. You can sit on your arses and starve to death if you want.'

'Don't be such a berk! Come back!' But Aaron was already squelching through the mud. 'He's crazy! Suppose he gets lost?'

'Ssh!' Tim whispered. 'He'll not go far. Listen.' Soon they heard him returning, the footsteps slower.

'Did you find it then?' Ray asked, genially.

'No.'

'Just walked off a little surplus temper, eh? What did you see? Sheep?'

'Don't,' Tim said.

'Why don't you just fuck off?' Aaron shouted. 'All of you!' He took the mint-cake out of his rucksack and began to eat it. Three pairs of eyes watched in accusing silence, and when he could no longer bear to ignore them he stuffed the remaining half-bar noisily into his possessions. Then he undressed, climbed into his bedding, and pretended to sleep.

53

'End of part one,' John said. 'Now for the adverts. Have you tried Suñer, the amazing new compass? Slips easily into the pocket *and* out of it. Useful in all weathers, including the strongest sun *rays*, ha-ha-ha. With it comes this *free* coupon for a *free* holiday on the sun-baked Costa del Glaramara—'

'I know,' Ray said, sighing. 'I know.'

'Which direction do we really want, Tim?'

'For Langdale, south a bit, then more or less east down the motorway . . .'

'Leaving Captain Scott's flag on the right by the South Pole?'

'. . . and I think we'd best go on our hunch about north being on the far side of the tarn.' Tim stared again at the map; it must, somehow, yield up the secret of where they were. The contour lines, the crags, the footpaths, the blue streams were already imprinted on his memory, but still there was no real clue.

'Do you think we should make a move?'

'Not yet. We could just wander about and get saturated for nothing.'

'Ron did have a point when he talked about starving,' Ray said.

'If we had to stop here all day and all night, and tomorrow as well, we might get hungry, but we wouldn't starve.'

'Charming,' Ray said, after a silence.

'There's biscuits, chocolate, apples, plenty of tea, and plenty of water in the tarn. I'll fill the kettle and make some tea. Give me something to do.'

He returned, dripping wet.

'If you left it outside,' John pointed out, 'It would soon fill itself.'

'Yes. So it would.'

'Regular little housewife she is,' Ray said. 'Must be the Irish Catholic in you. Tea with bog water.'

She? Did Ray mean anything? But he was grinning, quite amicably. Tim hoped his own face betrayed nothing. While they sipped their drinks he had to put up with a lot of banter about his religion. He was used to this, though never before from these two: the same kind of stupid remarks, however. Why weren't Catholics allowed into RE lessons? Miss Tweedsmuir was an earnest creature with spectacles who tried desperately to be as nice as pie to the rows of heathen in front of her. She would hardly be likely to deprave and corrupt, would she? And this rigmarole about Confession. All you had to do was reel off your sins to the priest, Father I had sex every night last week, say you were sorry and be free to go off and do it again as much as you wanted. And all those statues in the churches. Catholics worshipped statues, didn't they? You might just as well be a pagan on a South Sea Island.

'It's not like that at all,' Tim said.

'What is it like, then?' Ray wanted to know. This was the trap, he knew from past experience. You were led on into explaining, for example, the need to feel repentant without which Confession was quite useless, and this only meant more scorn. 'Go on,' said Ray. 'I really want to know. It's no battier than Anarcho-Syndicalism, I can assure you.' So he droned on, mechanically, aware of laughter in John's eyes, and he thought to himself with some astonishment, for it was perhaps the first time he had felt it, why does it sound like so much twaddle? It *is* twaddle. Isn't it? Force of habit. Not belief.

'After that mouthful,' John said, turning on the transistor, 'I need some music to flush me out.'

But it was news time, the local news. A fire in a house in Windermere, one woman dead. Hold-ups on the A66 owing to extensive roadworks at Bassenthwaite. Workington Council said last night that plans to build two new factories in the area had been shelved because of the economic crisis. 'Fears are being expressed for the safety of four teenagers on a walking holiday in the Lake District,' the news-reader said. 'They should have arrived in Langdale yesterday evening, but they have not been seen since Saturday, when they were heading for the south-west slopes of Great Gable. No search has yet been possible owing to the bad weather . . .'

'That's *us*!' cried Ray, appalled.

Half a dozen people were standing in the church porch. A man was taking photographs. A christening: the young woman in the centre was holding a tiny baby. Smart suits, long dresses, floppy hats. Tim and John waited until they had gone, then went inside. The vicar was writing a new name in the register of baptisms. It was not a particularly interesting church to the sightseer, but Tim was absorbed: all around, on the walls, and on the floor, were memorials to the Bampfylde family.

> Here lyeth John Bampfylde
> baronett who died April 24
> 1650 in the 40 yeare of his age

'So he didn't survive long, then! If we were him, we'd have only fifteen years left! I feel no intimations of mortality.'

'The inscription's odd,' John said. 'It doesn't make sense.' THE RIGHTEOUS PERISHETH AND NO MAN LAYETH IT TO HEART AND MERCIFULL MEN ARE TAKEN AWAY NONE CONSIDERING THAT THE RIGHTEOUS IS TAKEN AWAY FROM THE EVILL TO COME

'It sounds querulous,' Tim agreed. 'Whoever wrote it didn't approve of the Commonwealth, perhaps. It's a year after the King's execution. The Bampfyldes were Parliament men, though. What it is probably, yes, the son was a Royalist, the father not. The Civil War divided many families.'

'You're not lecturing your students now,' John said.

They walked through the gate at the end of the churchyard and along an avenue of enormous lime trees: spires of green and gold, ancient and beautiful. The sweet scent of the blossom was overpowering. Few people came this way; the grass between the two rows of trees was untrodden. The gardens, to the right, were derelict, a mass of weeds and untended shrubs. All that remained of a tennis court was the rusting wire cage that surrounded it. At the end of the avenue was Poltimore House. It was dying: loose tiles, cracked glass, peeling white stucco. Once it had been very handsome. Closed shutters on the insides of all the windows stopped anything intruding on its privacy.

'Do you ever hear from Ron these days?' Tim asked.

'A Christmas card, that's all. He's still in California.'

'And a millionaire.'

'He reminds me of someone who was in the charts when we were at school. Marty Kristian, was it?'

'Someone like that. I don't remember.'

The fields beyond the house had once been extensive parkland. Oaks and cedars of Lebanon, as old as the limes, stood singly in the middle of growing corn. A man and his two children were baling hay; they stared at John and Tim with curiosity, evidently wondering who these trespassers were. Three fields off, the summer traffic, en route for the holiday camps and caravan sites of Torbay, roared down the M5.

'It was once a hospital, Poltimore,' John said. 'It special-
ized in hernias, piles, rectal cancer, that sort of thing. It
became too expensive to run, and when the new hospital
opened in the city, it closed down.'

'It has atmosphere.' The wind made the trees sway
restlessly, a pleasing, melancholy sound. The uncut grass
was splashed with the red of poppies; thistles grew boldly in
an elegant garden urn. Tim thought of the nurses, off duty,
playing tennis, of Sir John Bampfylde and his family enter-
taining the commanders of the New Model.

'We should be getting back.' John looked at his watch.
'Lesley will have tea ready, and the children will be home
from school.'

'You, with a six-year-old daughter!'

'I was nineteen when Karen was born.'

'I remember. Are you happy?'

'Me and Lesley? Oh yes. Yes. Are you?'

'I don't have a wife and children, naturally. But I got
over thinking that left me out of things years ago. Yes, I'm
happy.'

'A pity Franco couldn't come.'

'He's in Spain for a fortnight.'

'Do you ever see him?'

'I had a drink with him last week. I often see him; we use
the same pub. He's still very militant, waving banners and
going on marches, writing articles and lobbying MPs.'
John laughed. 'What?'

'You. You and him. Ron. Me. Funny the way it all turns
out.'

A loud crack like a pistol-shot made them jump. A tile
had fallen from the roof and smashed to pieces. Birds flew
up in alarm from the grass and the flower-beds. It was a
place with a very special charge, Tim thought. The past

here was unquiet. If ghosts were real they would be in this house. The righteous perisheth and no man layeth it to heart: an epitaph for the whole troubled times, the troubled complex humans of both sides. They had never come to terms with the demons in themselves, did not know how to. A civil war derived not only from the inability of certain people to co-exist; it was an externalizing of the conflicts within the self. None of them had known that he could not possibly count himself with the righteous, that all men had an equal claim to that state. This house would always be restless.

CHAPTER FOUR

The tent smelled of stale air and unwashed bodies. It was home and sanctuary but also prison: one moment Tim was grateful for its warm protectiveness; the next he longed to be outside tramping over the mountains to Langdale. The news on the radio had horrified him. He felt like a small child surprised in the act of doing something extremely naughty: what would happen if it was repeated on the national network; suppose his parents heard it? His plight being made so public made him feel inexplicably guilty, as if, once again, he had let them down.

It was not the same for the others; he could sense this, even though John had said 'They'll be worried out of their minds!' and Ray had gasped 'My mother will be frantic!!'

'Of course they'll be frantic,' Aaron said. 'They're bound to be! Nothing we can do about it.'

Tim knew his control of the group was slipping away. Aaron sprawled in his sleeping-bag, sulking, Achilles in his tent. There was a feeling, emanating from Ray and John, that Tim's usefulness had finished, that he could no longer make decisions, that he had nothing new to offer. Just sit it out; the rain must cease and the clouds lift some time: they didn't like it. And he was sure they were thinking they might all slowly starve to death.

John and Ray discussed schemes and left him out. John thought aloud, scrutinized the map. He was all for doing something positive; find the way off the mountain: they could leave the tent where it was, and Aaron, and Tim if he didn't want to come, could stay till they returned. They must lay a trail behind them so they wouldn't get lost. How, Ray asked. Stones, John said; lift them from the ground, leave them in positions they'd remember, place them somehow so that they wouldn't mistake them for other bits of rock.

'Shame we haven't got a pot of paint,' said Ray, who was lukewarm about the idea.

'Don't be a twerp. Are you coming or not?'

'It's still raining,' Tim said.

'I'd rather get soaked than starve!'

'You say that because you're hungry, and dry.'

John, in answer, opened the tent flaps.

'Might as well give it a try,' Ray said, grudgingly.

'Oh, I'll come too.' Tim could no longer stand the inaction. He fingered the jeans he had worn yesterday; it was stupid to get both pairs of trousers soaked. They were still saturated.

'Wear Ron's shorts,' said Ray, watching him.

Aaron, lying on his back and gazing up at the tent roof, had no objection. 'Leave me some fags,' he said.

Tim put them on. They were damp and clammy, but they belonged to his beloved; he would have worn them if they had been dripping with water. In these, yesterday, Ron's legs had moved. It was hard not to bend down and kiss him in sheer gratitude.

The plan was pathetic, of course, even though it was good to be out of the stuffy intimacy of the tent. Every few yards they had to search for suitable stones which were not always easy to find. The further they ventured the less likely it was, Tim thought, that they would ever reach the tent again. The rain was the only sound, steady, drenching. His legs were cold, almost numb, like a swim in cold weather before drying onself. He began to admire the things of the landscape, the grass, the stones, for their ability to withstand. Once there was a sudden fleeting gap in the clouds and they had a brief glimpse of crags; they studied the map feverishly, but it was impossible to know which mountain the rocks belonged to. Once a sheep startled them, rising up and bolting off into the fog, a red smear and a mass of sodden dirty grey wool. Its bleat was a feeble whimper, as if it, too, had almost succumbed to the weather.

They discovered a way eventually that might be possible. There was no path, just heather, bilberry, tussocks of grass, but it was gently up and down, and avoided the sheer drops. The land was wetter, as if they were near the source of a stream. Then it became increasingly difficult. Their boots sank in thick dark mud, and it was a question of finding a stone or a dryer-looking patch to jump to. There was moss, and a thick growth of spongy plants, the colours of which looked almost unnaturally vivid, covering ground that was treacherous bog. John swore. His right leg had pierced the surface, up to his knee. He dragged himself out slowly; there was an ugly gurgling noise. His boot, sock and leg were black with freezing cold slime.

They stopped. They could not go on, nor in any direction except the way they had come. The marsh stretched to the edges of the cloud.

'Help!' Ray shouted at the top of his voice, and the others, when they realized it was not because he was in immediate difficulty, but more a general cry to the universe, joined in. 'Help! Help! . . . Help!!'

'Is there anybody there?' Tim yelled.

They listened. Only the faint echo of their own voices.

'We should have brought whistles,' Ray said.

'Oh . . . don't be so soft,' John said, wearily.

'Let's go home.' Ray turned, full of dejection.

'Home?'

'Back to the tent.'

'What about the expert's advice?' John looked at Tim. He, too, was beginning to know that he could not work miracles. Tim shook his head.

They retraced their steps, carefully examining the stones. They could be any old stones, Tim thought, but John kept up an air of confidence. The rain poured down. Some of him was quite dry, though that was small comfort. His arms, chest and shoulders were warm, part of his usual self, protected by his anorak. From the waist down he was as wet as if he was immersed in a cold bath, the least comfortable bit of him his feet; water sloshed and squelched between sock and the inside of the boot, yet sock, water, foot and boot were one, a tepid dirty swamp; it reminded him of the real marsh and its spongy bright excrescences, apologies for plants.

Perhaps we're all going to die, he thought gloomily, but without any sense of terror, for he didn't really believe they would. God will prevent us. Perhaps he should pray. Though that seemed melodramatic, almost cheating: why should God help them? The fiasco had been caused by a combination of the weather and Ray's carelessness in losing the compass. And because all of them had assumed that one compass would be sufficient. In any case horrendous disasters occurred throughout the world every minute and God didn't seem to do much about them: fire, flood, earthquakes; cars colliding; planes crashing; unwanted children. Maybe every minute of the day a homosexual was born. If you were born with it, that is. Did parents somehow create it? Not that it mattered. There was nothing wrong with being gay, he told himself without conviction. A man must be whatever he is, regardless of the odds. The odds, though, were overwhelming. Thou shalt not: God said it, parents said it, everybody else said it.

Perhaps there was no God. That would be a release! Freedom! This Catholic religion, tied to him like an old tin on a dog's tail. To be free of it, to throw it away like an old pair of knickers, to explore and enjoy everything he yearned for! Not that it would help the pain of loving Aaron. Making love to Ron would always be impossible. It was another tin it would be best to untie. How? No, life would not be worth living without Ron. Kill God, kill Aaron. Freedom! Somewhere surely, somewhere in this teeming universe of four thousand million people there must be a boy, a man, just as beautiful, whom he could love, who was homosexual, who would love him. A needle in a haystack, perhaps. Seek and ye shall find.

They found their way without any misfortune. John hesitated twice, trying to choose between one stone and another, and though Tim and Ray were doubtful about every one, at times silently but mostly aloud, the grey cone of the tent eventually took shape through the fog.

'I told you!' John shouted, triumphantly. He was leader now.

Aaron was still in his sleeping-bag, listening to the transistor. 'They corrected the earlier bulletin,' he said. 'We were last seen yesterday at Seathwaite. Proceeding in the direction of Sprinkling Tarn.'

'Help coming soon?' Ray asked anxiously.

'What do you think! If we can't find our way off this

64

bloody mountain, nobody's likely to know we're here, are they?'

John dropped his rucksack angrily. 'Fucking hell, Ron!'

'I was hungry.'

Tim and Ray looked in theirs. There was food still left, but Aaron had helped himself. 'If we're reduced to cannibalism,' John said, 'I'll stick a knife in you with pleasure.'

'There's more fat on Ray.'

John punched him on the mouth, hard. Aaron tried to retaliate, but it was not easy from a prone position in a sleeping-bag. John sat on his face, twisting his right arm.

'Apologize.'

'No.'

'Apologize!'

'All right, I'm sorry.'

'Doesn't give me back my orange,' Ray said.

'We'll eat the rest now,' said John. 'Then he can't steal any more. Fucking thief!'

Raisins, chocolate, apples, the last orange, biscuits, mint-cake. It was not a bad meal. 'Have a cheese sandwich,' Ray said, and flung it across the tent. 'It's stale. With my love.' Aaron ate it.

There is no God, Tim said to himself. I do not love Aaron. There is no God and I do not love Aaron. He remained unconvinced. There is a God and he will not punish me if I go to bed with another boy; I love Aaron but I will have to make love with someone else. He was still unconvinced. God is leaving me to die a slow and unpleasant death on a remote mountain miles from home. God does not care. I do not love Aaron because he is a petty thief, a spoiled self-centred brat. He is not a sungod, not any more. Aaron is not worth my love. But God is still here, and so is Aaron. There must be a way out of this! If there

65

isn't I shall die anyway; not literally, but here, inside, where it matters.

There is a way out and I know it. Love another and make love together, knowing that though we don't have God's blessing there is at least His vast indifference. I have only to make myself believe it.

If not, I shall die; here, inside, where it matters.

'Can I come in?' It was Saint-Hill. Tim, amazed, dropped Anthony's lute. 'Don't stand there gaping!'

He rushed to the door and bolted it. 'How—'

'Easy. My turnkey is a Parliamentarian. Very well-known a while ago for his views, but since the last siege he has professed a fanatical support for the King, in order not to lose his employment, I assume. It was quite simple. When nobody was looking he unlocked my cell and let me out.'

'And you a Royalist.'

'Yes. It's all becoming rather complicated.'

'Anthony is not here.'

'I know. I hid where I could watch, and waited until I saw him leave. You're surprised, but you know perfectly well he would not give me shelter.'

'Then how can I?'

Saint-Hill smiled. 'Not in here, of course.' He seemed tired, but otherwise fitter than when Tim found him near Poltimore. He needed a shave, but he had managed to comb his hair and change his clothes.

'Where then?'

'The tower of Holy Trinity. Anthony has a key.'

Tim crossed the room and picked it up from the window-sill. 'There's another key. The sexton has it.'

'We both know the sexton. It will be all right.'

66

'How are your wounds?'

'Better.'

Tim led the way out, onto the battlements, and opened the door of the tower. A spiral staircase led into the bell-chamber. No-one had been up there for years; it was thick with dust and cobwebs. There were no bells. There had once been four, but they had been taken down and placed in St Kieran's: Holy Trinity was a poor parish, and the few things of value its church possessed had been removed by the Puritans before the Royalists' successful siege in 1643. The authorities had not bothered themselves to see that they were returned.

'Later on please bring me something to eat,' Saint-Hill begged. 'I would be most grateful.'

'Of course. I promise.'

There was little meat and only a few vegetables in the upstairs room. The future was difficult to predict: it would be necessary to go out foraging, though the supplies on the nearest farms had already been taken. Breaking through the enemy's lines might be the only way of surviving. Anthony had been too greedy; he had sold off most of the food and pocketed the money.

A stew, Tim decided, was the best idea: it made it more difficult for Anthony to notice that anything was missing. 'You're a good cook,' said Saint-Hill, with a sigh, as if he could eat it all over again.

'I can't spare more. He will guess.'

'I understand.' Saint-Hill nodded. 'Does anyone know that I'm here?'

'No-one at all.'

'Good.' He walked across the room, then peered out of the window. 'I'm bored,' he said. 'There's nothing to do, no-one to talk to except spiders. I wish I had a book to read. Can you bring me one of Anthony's?'

'I daren't.'

'I suppose not.' Saint-Hill evidently wished to prolong the conversation, but Tim feared he would be missed, and he did not want Anthony to become suspicious. He made his way down the staircase. A man was standing in the shadows by the door.

It was Jake. 'Our friend has eaten well?' he asked.

'You made me jump out of my skin!'

'Walk along the wall with me; there's something I want to show you.'

'I can't.'

The door of the gatehouse opened and Anthony emerged. 'So that's where you are,' he said.

'I'm taking him to see the new wonders,' Jake explained.

Anthony seemed to have no suspicions about Saint-Hill's presence in the tower. 'The stew was excellent,' he said. 'I'll leave yours over the fire for when you come back.' He went inside.

As far as he was concerned, Jake said, Saint-Hill could stay in the tower until the siege was over. He'd seen the man arrive and guessed where his hiding-place would be. People like that were harmless. They should be left alone for they hurt no-one.

'What are the new wonders?' Tim asked.

'All in good time.'

The wall sloped steeply downhill near the south-west corner of the city. There was a fine view of the river; the quay, of course, was deserted: not one ship rode at anchor, for since the Roundheads had stopped up this highway of Exeter's trade by sinking five vessels at Topsham, the port had been at a standstill.

The west gate was not the most massive and imposing of all the city's entrances, but it had the greatest quantity of fortifications; it had been built in an age when the main threat to life was thought to be from the west: in the distance lay the wilderness of Dartmoor and, beyond, Cornwall, the home of Celtic people with outlandish speech and uncertain loyalties. From the gatehouse to the river there was swamp. The bridge had changed little since medieval times: it was narrow and constructed of many small arches through which the water flowed swiftly. On each end were houses, in ruins now, and on the city side stood St Edmund's church, its slender tower like a sentinel. The middle section of the bridge had been blown up by Goring's cavalry.

'Look at the far side of the river,' Jake said.

In the growing dusk there were camp fires the whole length of the opposite bank, and around them men sat, or walked aimlessly, or cooked. There was a huge army of tents, and horses tethered to posts, hundred of horses, thousands of men. 'What is it?' Tim asked, noticing that the Royalist guns on the walls and the gatehouse roof, which were pointing directly across the river, were silent. 'Has Goring returned to lift the siege?'

Jake laughed. 'It's Cromwell.'

'*Cromwell!* How does he dare to come so close? Why are our guns not firing?'

'Berkeley has agreed to surrender the city.'

'What are they waiting for?'

'These things take time. Berkeley is still at Poltimore, and the entry into the city has to be arranged. You don't expect the New Model to surge in like some rowdy drunken mob? Fairfax will want the surrender to be an orderly parade, and so some organization is necessary. But it is

69

whispered about that at twelve noon tomorrow the gates
will be opened.'

Tim was silent, wondering what this would mean for
him. He rejoiced at the thought of a Parliament victory,
but his own future was a question mark. It depended to
some extent on Anthony, Saint-Hill, and perhaps Jake
also: there were ambiguities in these three men, and his
own safety depended on whether their roles in the siege
were made any clearer. 'I don't know what to think,' he
said.

'I'll leave you to think, then,' said Jake. 'I have many
things to do.'

'In the siege of Paris the inhabitants ate cats and dogs,'
Aaron said. 'Afterwards, rats. A good fat rat cost several
francs.' He had been watching, the previous week, a television programme on the Commune.

'At Leningrad they ran out of rats,' said Ray. Like Tim
he was studying History for 'A' level. 'They stewed old
leather boots to make broth. At the Alcázar—'

'What's the Alcázar?' Tim asked.

'A fortress near Toledo. The rebels were besieged in
it and Franco relieved it, unfortunately. It was strange.
Our men threw food and cigarettes in to the rebel troops,
and at the same time tried to blow the whole place to
bits.'

It was nearly midnight. They had gone to bed but no-
one could sleep; they were too hungry. They had not eaten
since late morning, and all they had left to drink was
milkless tea. Time hung heavily, and the atmosphere was
made more gloomy by the repeated news bulletins. Yet no-
one wished to turn the radio off; it assured them that
somewhere outside the tent there was a civilized existence

that had not forgotten them. They wondered privately, however, how long it would take to starve to death, though no-one voiced it aloud. At about nine o'clock the rain had stopped, so there was hope, even if it was too dark to do anything until morning.

Aaron's theft of the food seemed to have been forgiven. There was too much in him that attracted the others, his gut reactions, his self-sufficiency. He had gone out on his own during the afternoon, complaining of the fetid atmosphere of the tent, and bathed in the tarn. It was bitterly cold, he said when he returned, shivering, but worth it; he felt greatly refreshed, and when he had dried himself he did twenty press-ups, scattering everybody's belongings in the process. He appeared to think nothing of being naked in such close proximity to the others: maybe, Tim thought, because he knew his body was worth being seen, but it wasn't quite that; it was an absence of any sense that nudity was embarrassing. Tim could never have sat there with no clothes on. Nor, probably, could John and Ray. It was absurd, he thought, this shame in front of a visible sign of adulthood; Aaron's acceptance of it was a mark of a certain maturity he did not possess himself. Ray called him a flasher, and Aaron replied that it was a more interesting nickname than Franco.

John passed the time reading *Confessions of a Window Cleaner*; 'a good laugh,' he said when Ray asked what he thought of it.

'Is it real?' Tim wanted to know. He had skipped through it earlier, reading the passages where the book fell open: it offended everything he felt about love and sex.

'It's quite stimulating.'

'If it's real,' Aaron said, 'he's luckier than I've been, or anyone else I've ever heard of.'

'It's a laugh,' John repeated. 'People don't behave like that.'

'How do you know?'

'Well, they don't. My dad's mate is a window cleaner, and he had to rescue a woman once who'd locked herself in the lavatory. She couldn't get out. But all he got for his trouble was a cup of tea.'

'That's all you know.'

'Ah, come on.'

'You don't know!'

'No,' said John, yawning, bored with the conversation.

'The women in the book are just objects,' Tim said. 'Sexual receptacles.'

'Tim doesn't love women,' Aaron said.

John laughed. 'Then we'd better all watch ourselves. I'm going to bed.' Silence followed this. They don't really mind; that's the extraordinary thing, Tim said to himself, as he lay in his sleeping-bag, later, listening to Ray talking about the siege of the Alcázar. He wished he did love women: it would make life much less difficult. Everything else would then be in harmony. It would be so much easier to live, not wasting hours and hours in this neurotic self-analysis. Yet he was accepted by these three, for these moments in time. He was grateful. Another voice inside said it was absurd to be grateful, almost a betrayal. It was Uncle Tom-ism. Why shouldn't Aaron be equally grateful that he, Tim, accepted, without comment, the sungod's heterosexuality? Black people didn't exactly tug forelocks to all the whites in this country. Most of them—he hoped it was most of them—were proud to be Kenyan or Nigerian or whatever. The same went for Jews. And Catholics. (That was an irony!) 'When we're out in the streets,' Father Sullivan said, years ago, at the start of the Corpus

Christi procession, 'remember we're Catholics. Be proud to show to all those people, Protestants, atheists and the like, who will stop and stare and may well be laughing at you, that you believe in the Holy Catholic Church!' So why shouldn't homosexuals think similarly?

Ave! Ave! Ave Maria! It was the day of his first Communion. Aged seven. Little girls with white veils, little boys with white bands on their arms. All singing, round the streets, in a procession of quite respectable size someone said. The grown-ups at the back holding banners: the Guild of the Blessed Sacrament, the Legion of Mary. People had stared, harmless housewives with shopping-baskets. It made him feel foolish. *Ave! Ave! Ave Maria!* His mother with her folding Kodak, taking his photograph.

John and Aaron were asleep, their breathing even and restful. Ray tossed and turned. In the Spain he hated, in every town and village, on the feast of Corpus Christi, *Ave! Ave! Ave Maria!*

Ray got up and went outside. Tim heard him pee. Drenching already sodden ground. He came back, shone the torch at Tim. 'Are you awake?'

'Yes.'

'Can I shift my sleeping-bag nearer?'

'Why?'

'I'm cold.'

'All right.' Though Tim could not follow the logic. Ray moved closer. The side of his sleeping-bag, Tim noticed, was unzipped. What was all this about? Ray switched the torch off.

'Tim.'

'Yes.'

'Are you . . . what Ron says?'

Why not admit, he thought with beating heart. The

73

question didn't sound unkindly, and, anyway, Ray knew. There was nothing to lose. 'Yes.'

'So am I.'

'What!!'

'Sssh! Don't wake them up!'

'But . . . you never . . . I mean, you and Ron, your talk of girls . . . Ray, is this a joke?'

'No, it certainly isn't a joke!'

'But . . . I don't understand.'

'I'll explain, another time, not now. It would take ages; the others might wake up.' He was unzipping Tim's sleeping-bag.

'No.'

'Why not?'

'It's wrong.'

'Nonsense.' Ray's hand was touching him, softly stroking his skin. This *can't* be happening! It's a dream! I'll wake up in a sweat, and Ray's sleeping-bag will be where it always is, Ray in it, asleep. Wrong, wrong: mortal sin, God's anger. The fires of Hell, an eternity of it unless there is repentance. Father Sullivan, shocked, on the other side of the confession grille. Wrong, too: Ray is not ugly, but I don't love Ray. I couldn't kiss him. It would be easier, he decided with almost Jesuitical precision, to repent it with Ray. Afterwards he would feel only remorse, disgust. With Aaron it would be much more difficult to experience regret, impossible in fact: he would in that case for ever be cut off from God. This, with Ray; it was nothing, just another boy tossing him off.

'No.' But it sounded feeble.

'You're all screwed up, Tim. You're crying out for it; I've seen it in your eyes. You're so frustrated!'

'Maybe. But not for you.'

'Ron.'

'Yes.'

'I'd love it with him too. But it's useless, begging for the impossible.'

'It's stopped me sinning.'

'Sin! That's absurd!'

'It isn't.'

'You're so screwed up. Have you never done it before?'

'Only by myself.' Losing my virginity. An appalling way to lose it, sinning with someone I don't fancy. But he was shaking with excitement.

'I'm coming in with you.'

'No.'

Ray's legs on his, his body on top of him.

CHAPTER FIVE

All four gates of the city were open, but Fairfax had decided that his conquering army should enter from the east. Cromwell, still obliging his commander-in-chief, obeyed orders and remained on the far side of the river, and his men spent the day repairing the blown-up section of the bridge. Sir Hardress Waller came through the south gate. It had been open since dawn, but there was no sign of Anthony. When Tim woke the other half of the bed was empty, but it looked as if he intended to return, for he had not removed any of his possessions.

Tim walked with Jake up to the High Street, and from there to Rougemont Castle, the headquarters of the garrison and the civil administration. Berkeley, it was thought, would officially hand over the city when Fairfax arrived at the castle; a proclamation would be read out from the steps giving the terms of surrender. The streets were filled with people. Puritan sympathizers who had remained quietly in their homes for months, and those released from gaol that morning, felt free to move about, and the expressions on their faces reflected their happiness; at last a cruel and arbitrary despotism had been defeated. It was no wild carnival of celebration, however; their religious beliefs prohibited any vain enjoyment. They simply went about their business, greeting old friends not seen for weeks, trying to impress Royalist neighbours (who mostly remained indoors watching from upper windows) that they were honest, sober, and industrious citizens.

Tim and Jake found a place from which they could view the proceedings, high up on a wall that marked the edge of the castle gardens. Shortly after noon the first soldiers of the New Model marched into the city. They could not be seen from where Tim sat, but the sound of tramping feet and the thump of drums drew closer and closer, followed by the clopping of horses' hooves. Most of the troops dispersed to the main cross-roads, to the houses of the more notorious Cavaliers, and to strategic positions on the walls and the roofs of the gates. Foot-soldiers appeared in the castle grounds, then the cavalry, and finally, on a white horse, Sir Thomas Fairfax himself.

There was a long silence, and the great concourse of people watched and waited.

Sir John Berkeley emerged, alone. Fairfax dismounted and climbed the steps. The two opposing commanders, relentless enemies for so many years, politely doffed their hats to each other. Berkeley handed over the keys of the city, the keys of the castle. Fairfax summoned a herald, who, after a fanfare on his trumpet, read out the surrender terms. The whole city, its castle and fortifications, and all weapons, supplies and provisions were to be handed over to the officers and men of the New Model. The Princess Henrietta Maria and her household were free to go wherever the King should decide. The Royalist garrison was to leave as soon as the reading of the proclamation was finished; they could go to their own homes or depart for the continent. Citizens who were known to have supported the King would be fined, but their property would not be confiscated. The cathedral, the city churches and their clergy, were granted special terms of protection. (There was some muttering in the crowd at this point; this edict was not popular: Dissenters remembered their own chapels, locked up or destroyed by fire.) All charters, property and privileges enjoyed by the people of Exeter and its corporation were to be safeguarded for the future. There would be no prisoners and no hostages.

Such terms were generous beyond the wildest expectations of even the most optimistic of Royalist supporters. 'He can afford to be generous,' Jake said, 'but it doesn't mean there won't be reprisals. There's many an old score to be paid off.' Tim gazed at Fairfax. Slight in build, modest in appearance, his face stern. He had an air about him that suggested that, if he had needed to, he could have driven a much harder bargain.

A horse was fetched for Berkeley and a way cleared through the crowd. The ex-Governor raised his hat once more, and rode out of the city. The remnant of the Royalist cavalry followed, then their infantry. Anthony was not among them.

Fairfax returned to his horse and entered the castle, accompanied by several of his officers. A great cheer went up from the crowd.

'It's peace!' Tim shouted. 'We're free!' He felt a surge of joy. 'We can release Saint-Hill!'

'Yes, we can do that,' Jake answered.

'What's wrong?'

'The next few days will show how free we really are.'

'But you heard the proclamation!'

'Just wait, that's all.'

'Hush! Ssh, ssh! They'll wake up!' The whisper roared

in his ear. Tongues touching. Tenderness. Ray uncoiling, a deep satisfied sigh, resting in his arms, trusting him like a baby would trust a mother. The beating of his heart. Falling asleep.

Tim and Jake were surprised by the raucous din coming from inside the cathedral. At the west door an elderly clergyman, held back by two men, was shouting angrily at a group of soldiers lolling against the wall of St Mary Major. 'Are these our special terms of protection?' he cried. 'Stop them! Stop them!' But the soldiers only laughed.

'Shall we see what's happening?' Jake suggested.

'Is it safe?'

Jake looked scornful. He walked up to one of the soldiers and spoke to him. The man, apparently, had no objection, and Jake went into the cathedral. Tim followed. The Puritans had probably indulged in worse orgies of destruction than this; the troops of the New Model were not decapitating the corbels, or throwing whitewash at the wall-paintings, or smashing up what might be considered graven images. They were dismantling the organ, and piling the wood on to a cart. A horse waited patiently in the shafts. Tim had never seen a horse inside a church; it was grotesquely out of place, a repulsive insult. The organ pipes were being stacked in a corner, presumably to await collection when the load of wood had been delivered. But things were getting out of hand, and the officer in charge merely stood by and smiled. The men had picked up some of the smaller pipes and were blowing a deafening cacophony of rude noises out of them. A few louts had decorated their heads and bodies with altar cloths, copes and chasubles; one even dared to wear the Bishop's mitre, tilted

79

back at a rakish angle. They started to dance down the nave and out of the west door.

The virger, an old man with white hair, stood in the shadows and watched. He was far too terrified to intervene, even though the desecration of the building he had loved and worked in for years scandalized him as nothing in the whole of his previous life had done. 'They are going to build a brick wall at the crossing!' he whispered to Tim. He was trembling. 'This has been the House of God for five hundred years, and they are destroying it! A brick wall at the crossing, where the organ stood! So they can have two temples, yes, temples, for I will not call their profane tabernacles places of worship!'

The officer strolled nonchalantly down the nave. 'Stop muttering, old man,' he said. 'Go down on your knees and give thanks to God. What is the usual behaviour of victorious armies, eh? They loot, burn, rape, and kill. You will see no such conduct from the New Model.' He walked on, a supercilious grin on his face.

'Come on,' said Jake, and they left the old virger to tidy up as best he could. Across Cathedral Yard wove the strange procession of dancing men; it was like a parody of some ancient ritual: the gawky steps of the dance, the shrieks and howls from the organ pipes, the ecclesiastical robes fluttering in the breeze. Passers-by stopped, stared, and laughed; or else hurried away, shocked and horrified, thus betraying their sympathies for all to see. The Bishop's mitre was lying in the mud. Tim picked it up.

'Drop it!' Jake said. 'At once!'

'Why?'

'Don't be a fool! Drop it!'

He let it fall, reluctantly. Though he had little time for the pretensions of bishops (they were, every one of them, of the King's persuasion) the mitre was precious and beautiful. It would now be left to rot, like some old dish-cloth.

They arrived at Holy Trinity and unlocked the door of the tower. Saint-Hill was eager for news, and overjoyed to hear that their would be no prisoners or hostages. 'Freedom! Fairfax is a greater man than any on the King's side!'

'He had you whipped,' Tim pointed out.

'He had no option. He was trying to create something much more charitable, much more magnanimous, than anything I could offer him. I came at the worst possible moment. He had to present a show of strength in front of Berkeley, did he not? If Berkeley had thought him weak, his plans might not have succeeded so well.'

Tim found the logic of this tortuous, but he made no comment. 'Have you seen Anthony?' he asked.

'No.'

'Here he is now.' Jake was looking out of the window in the direction of the gatehouse. He turned, and said, with surprise and alarm in his voice, 'He's just loaded his pistol!' They heard the door open below.

Rain, a high wind and swirling fog when they woke. To try and move off the mountain was impossible. An early news bulletin said that if the four boys were still alive ('We are!' they shouted) they should not attempt to leave wherever they had camped; the safest thing was to wait till the weather changed. There was an interview with Mrs Hewitt. Low, hurried voice, Suffolk accent, pressing the emotions down inside by sheer will-power. John put his hands over his eyes. Her son was a good boy, very sensible, not one to take risks. There was no evidence that there had been an accident; it was quite probable the boys were sheltering in their tent, just waiting for the cloud to lift. John, if you're listening, and Mrs Suñer says Ray took his transistor, keep your chin up. There'll be a hot drink waiting for you and your favourite dinner.

John threw himself on to his sleeping-bag.

The four mothers were staying at a hotel in Ambleside. They all sent their love; don't give up hope for they hadn't: keep warm and wrap up well.

They looked at each other, moved beyond words by distress. Eventually Ray said 'What a sodding flop it all is,' and Aaron replied, in a choked voice, 'Yes, isn't it.' John, his eyes wet, said 'If we get out of this we'll all meet on Saturday night at home. We'll have the biggest piss-up the town's ever seen. Just the four of us. I feel . . . we have such a bond between us.'

They nodded, agreeing. 'If only I wasn't so bloody hungry!' Aaron said.

By mid-afternoon they had not eaten for twenty-four hours, Ray gloomily told them. There was plenty of warm weak tea, and they drank it by the gallon; but they were beginning to feel light-headed. They spent much of the day in their sleeping-bags, listening to Radio One, not talking much.

'Tea's run out,' Tim said, late in the evening. 'Water, hot or cold. That's all now.'

'I read somewhere about a man in a mine disaster,' Aaron said. 'He was buried alive for a month. Falling rocks had blocked the tunnel. A month he lived, and that was because he drank the water trickling down the walls.'

No-one answered. The wind howled; the cloud rushed by but it did not lift.

Tim was morose all day, lost in himself. The added pain of his mother anxiously waiting at Ambleside hardly affected him. He longed to talk to Ray, but it was not possible. Ray behaved as he always did, gave no hint of what had happened last night. He wondered for a moment if it had been a dream. When he woke the sleeping-bag was in its usual place and Ray was curled up in it. Tim couldn't remember him leaving. Now there was the disgust he had expected, not just for allowing himself to do it, but for actually enjoying it. It didn't even have the excuse that he loved Ray, that he had longed for ages to make love with him. It had been pure lust, and he had enjoyed it. Was it? It was tender, and sweet, too. Something more complex than he had thought, but not love, not the love that might be the only justification that, inside himself, would suffice, even if the Church called it mortal sin. The Church did not even bother to make a distinction between love and lust. He told himself he would refuse if Ray asked again; he would be strong, fight it: but he knew it would be a battle. One mortal sin was enough to send him to Hell. A second could not make it worse. The hanged-for-a-sheep-or-a-lamb syndrome.

Confession on Saturday if they survived, did not die of hunger. If he did die, he would go to Hell. He stared at this fact for a while, then flatly rejected it. It was like the Aborigines' reaction to their first sight of Captain Cook: so unbelievable that it couldn't be so, wasn't really there. If a flying saucer full of little green Martians landed in the school playground, who would believe their own eyes? God was not that merciless. The Church was wrong. Who was it compared the Catholic religion to a house of cards? Take one away and the whole thing collapses. It's a structure so logical (accepting, that is, the illogical premise of faith) right down to its last tiny detail, that, if you remove one minute piece, it all begins to unravel. He knew he had started this perilous procedure, started it just now, for the first time. It was nothing to do with if, or perhaps, or but: he flatly rejected as impossible that he, if he died before he next went to Confession, would be cut off and cast into Hell.

And he would go to Confession. The cards don't fall that quickly; the knitting takes a while to unravel into a mass of wool. Bless me, Father, for I have sinned. It would be easier, not so embarrassing, to find a church in another town. There was only the one at home, Our Lady Immaculate. Father Sullivan and Father Quinlan. They knew him too well. The Reverend Patrick Sullivan had baptized him seventeen years ago; from the Reverend Dermot Quinlan he had received his first Communion. One of them (which?) would soon know he was homosexual.

How long is it since your last confession?

Three weeks.

What do you have to tell me?

I've told lies. I've disobeyed my parents. I haven't always said my prayers at night. I've had . . . impure thoughts.

How often have you had these thoughts?

Occasionally. And . . . impure deeds.

By yourself?

Yes.

How many times?

I don't know. (How many times! What difference does it make? Why does he need to know?)

Once a week? Three times? (Pause.) Every night?

Once (it might be twice, perhaps, or three times before Saturday next) with somebody else.

A girl?

No.

(Pause.) You must try hard to give up this sin, or it will

84

destroy you. It can lead to madness. (Rubbish! If that was true, there would be no boys in the sixth form, or the fifth or fourth, and not very many in the third year either. They'd all be in a lunatic asylum.) It kills all moral fibre; it saps the strength. Are you sorry for these, and all your other sins?

Now this is the real trap, the one from which there is no escape. If I say I'm sorry and I don't mean it, I will be damned even more in God's eyes than I am already. Confession doesn't work unless there is genuine repentance. And Communion in a state of mortal sin . . . unthinkable. If I say no, then he will refuse me absolution until I am sorry. I think, Father . . . I may be tempted again.

You must fight it. Fight it with all your strength.

The temptation is hard to resist, Father. I . . . enjoyed it. (No, he could never bring himself to say such a thing!)

With the other boy?

Yes.

But are you sorry for what you've done?

(Pause.) I . . . don't know, Father.

I can't absolve you unless you are, unless you feel within yourself that you'll make a real effort not to commit these sins again. Do you understand that?

Yes.

When you're in a state of temptation think of our Saviour who died on the Cross for us; think of His mother, the Blessed Virgin Mary. Ask for their help; they *will* help you.

Yes, Father.

Now go, and come back to me when you think you can. Pray for me.

It wouldn't run quite like that, of course. Between the two of them they'd work out some formula; Father Quinlan (he was the easier, inclined to be absent-minded, particularly if he was looking forward to a day off with the scouts, or supervising a youth club social) would probably assume from the fact that he was there, kneeling and confessing his sins, that he was sorry anyway, and not press the point. But whatever happened, it would be a patched-up shoddy affair, indecent almost. More so than last night. That hadn't been indecent! Ray falling asleep in his arms: the trust of it.

> I, like an usurpt town, to another due,
> Labour to admit you, but, oh, to no end

These 'A' level texts, bits and bobs of them, apt and comforting. Nor ever chaste except you ravish mee: i.e. my true self, at peace, fulfilled, rejecting all doctrines, dogmas, tenets and texts that say what I am is evil.

'You're very preoccupied,' said Aaron. 'Snap out of it.'

He smiled. 'I'll try.'

'I've just asked you, twice, if you'd like to play chess. I've already beaten John and Ray; they're in a different class. A lower class.'

'I'll thrash you.' He suddenly felt happier.

'With whose army? All the pouffs?'

'In serried ranks assembled.'

Aaron laughed.

That was all there was, a plaque in dire need of cleaning, on a modern wall. *Site of south gate. King Henry VI here entered the city 16 July 1452. For centuries a prison. Demolished 1819.* According to the guide-book it had been removed for a road improvement scheme, and this had also meant destroying Holy Trinity: one wall of the church, as Tim knew, was a wall of the gatehouse. But the church had been resurrected whereas the gate had not; or, rather, a grotesque mock Gothic edifice now stood there, its proportions dismal, its windows mean, and the superstructure on its roof—it could in no way be called a tower—was not sure if it was functioning as a turret or an imitation chimney. It seemed, however, that this horror would soon pass into oblivion, for its entrance was boarded up with sheets of corrugated iron; plaster was falling from its walls, and buddleia sprouted in every crack. It would be left to decay, Tim imagined, until it was beyond repair, then the Council would knock it down, having declared it 'unsafe'. And there would not be, in its place, a third Holy Trinity.

Exeter was particularly good at demolishing 'unsafe' buildings, John said. Tim looked at the huge pile of rubble beyond the church. Until last week this had been a row of seventeenth-century houses, the oldest of which dated from just after the Civil War. The Council had wanted to construct a fly-over, and the houses were in the way; so they bought up the whole terrace, then decided against the fly-over. Years of neglect and vandalism had made the buildings dangerous, therefore down they had come. 'There was a great deal of protest about it,' John said. 'Articles in the newspapers and so on, but nothing can deflect our glorious Council from its mighty purposes.'

Bulldozers were shifting the rubble. A fire blazed, burning up all the old wood. 'Nothing remains,' Tim said.

'Of what?'

'This place. As it was.'

'There's the city walls.'

It was not possible to walk on the top of them now; there were no steps, and, besides, the Inner Bypass had necessitated the removal of a large chunk of the ancient fortifications: through a space, wider than a gatehouse would have been, cars and lorries surged.

'A blighted area,' Tim said. 'The abomination of desolation.'

'Yes. People say the Council has pulled down more of Exeter than the Germans bombed in the war.'

Even though there was no fly-over, there was a vast road complex, bristling with double yellow lines, traffic lights and direction signs. Cars stopped, moved forward, stopped again. In the middle was a piece of waste ground, where houses had stood long ago. It was now a parking lot, and at the far end was a modern pub.

'I'll leave you,' said John. 'I have to pick Lesley up.'

'Strange you came to live in Exeter.'

'Why?'

'So far from home.'

'Not so far as Ron went. Yes, four years we've been here now.'

'I think I'll have a drink in that pub. What is it?'

'The Acorn.'

'Well . . . I'll see you later.'

Tim dodged in and out of the traffic. He shouldn't have come, he kept thinking; it was all a bitter disappointment. Still, what did he expect? Exeter as it was in 1646? Fairfax issuing orders from the castle? At least some trace, some clue. But there was nothing, only these few sections of the walls. They looked unwanted, almost a nuisance, while the twentieth century rushed by, intent on its own frenetic business. The city's coat of arms, which he had seen on the plaque, had a motto that was unintentionally ironic: 'Semper Fidelis'. He hoped Ray, on his visit to the Alcázar, was finding something more rewarding. He'd ask Ray to dinner next week, and they could compare notes.

It was quite mad; perhaps they were delirious from lack

88

of food. When Aaron announced that he was going to swim in the tarn again, they all followed. Four naked youths, sloshing through mud in the pouring rain, yelling wild war-cries, screaming with laughter, diving into freezing cold water, shouting obscenities at the tops of their voices, hurling handfuls of mud, daubing each other with slime. Crazy! Then a final plunge to get clean, and a race back to the tent for towels, and jumping into the sleeping-bags for warmth to restore life. Giggling, shivering, teeth chattering. Their faces were blue and half-drowned, their skin shrunk and goose-pimpled. Tim ached from head to foot with the cold. But warmth, soon enough, seeped through, and his body relaxed. He felt exhilarated; refreshed, as Aaron had said yesterday. Yesterday, Tim would never have done this.

John had voiced it aloud: we have such a bond between us. 'Where shall we go for this piss-up?' Aaron asked.

'A five-course dinner,' Tim suggested. 'The Clarence.' 'Mario's.'

'None of your Italian muck,' Ray said. 'What about the Spanish restaurant, La Pasionaria? The proprietor's a mate of my dad's. Paella!'

'Not Spanish muck, either,' John said. 'The Clarence.'

'And booze,' said Aaron. 'Lots of vino.'

'And a disco afterwards.'

'No, not a disco. This is for us. Us four only.'

'Back to my house,' Tim said, 'and listen to records.'

'Why not? We've never been there,' Aaron said.

It was settled. Whatever happened, Tim thought, he had three real friends. For the time being. When—if—they returned to normal life, maybe the comradeship might slowly disappear. John and Aaron would drift back to the

89

routines of their usual existence, Ray . . . nothing would ever be the same again with Ray.

'Can't you turn the transistor up?' Aaron asked.

'Battery's going,' Ray said. 'By tomorrow it will be kaput.'

'Turn it off, then. We won't get any more news now.'

'I hope they don't interview *my* mother.'

The thought of the four women anxiously waiting at Ambleside made them all silent and depressed, and the silence meant they could not divert themselves from their hunger; it was becoming acute now, a gnawing griping pain inside. There was constant excess saliva in Tim's mouth, worsened by the visions of food that would not stop passing in front of his eyes. Once he really imagined he saw a frying-pan, sizzling with bacon, eggs, sausages, tomatoes and mushrooms: I'm going weak in the head, he thought; that was an hallucination. Peaches. Roast beef. Cheese: Brie, Cheddar, Danish blue. Golden syrup pudding. His stomach had a life of its own; it was like horny fingers clenching and unclenching.

It was astonishing what Ray had said: 'So am I.' Tim had never once suspected it. Was it true? Was it only because he was feeling randy and thinking that that was the best thing to say to get Tim to agree? No. He had sounded sincere. Nothing about him had previously suggested he was like that. He was a pretend-man even more than Tim. Tim knew other boys thought *he* was queer; he didn't like games, didn't go out with girls and usually ignored them at school, kept much to himself. But Ray! He was Aaron's lieutenant, looked up to him, executed his orders; he often went out with girls, sometimes as a foursome with Ron and partner, danced at discos. Only the other night, at the pub at Borrowdale, he had been chatting up that blonde from the youth hostel. And it was Ray, that afternoon last week, in the classroom, who had objected the most about Tim coming on this trip. Incredible! He was far worse a pretend-man, then; covering up every trace of it, a life of total deceit and hypocrisy. At least Tim didn't go to such lengths. Not that he exactly announced 'I'm homosexual' to all and sundry, but, if he suspected other people had guessed, he didn't alter his behaviour to prove he wasn't.

If you could tell someone was homosexual by their manner of dress, or behaviour, the way they walked (and Tim already doubted this; he was convinced he was in no way effeminate himself), then Ray was living proof that such a theory was nonsense. Physically tough and mature, deep bass voice, hairy (though that, of course, might be simply because he was Spanish), a very animal boy: good at all games, first eleven football, like Ron. Totally masculine. Tim thought hard: no, he was sure there was nothing he had missed in Ray that indicated what he was.

And then the question of parents, upbringing. Tim had read things on the subject, searching for reassurances and explanations, and the books usually said it was caused by one's mother wearing the trousers, or being too loving and over-protective, or Dad being absent or a weak character. It didn't altogether fit his own family, though he could see a few parallels. He didn't love either of his parents much, but that just made him feel guilty: he couldn't see why it should force him to prefer a man, sexually. Maybe one day it would all be clearer; growing up constantly involved new insights, not always pleasant ones, into Mum and Dad. Perhaps eventually he would be able to see how this theory included his own upbringing. Or not, as the case might be. His mother's desires to see him succeed, educationally, he thought pathetic rather than bossy (though it didn't stop him acting out her wishes) and Dad could certainly throw his weight around if he wanted to. Fold your flannel in four. Even at seventeen, a year off legal adulthood, it was still more than he felt his life was worth to disobey.

He didn't know the Suñer family of course, but he had seen them once, and the fanatical grandparents, at Open Day. He hadn't taken a lot of notice of them, but he did remember Ray showing his father around. Just like any other father and son. Nothing had registered, but he hadn't been looking for clues then. Ray certainly seemed very proud of his family, a close-knit tribe Tim imagined, like immigrants usually were: he talked far more about them than people at school normally did, ignoring, for the most part, all the insults about Spain. No. No clues. If only they could talk! His curiosity was intense; the day had passed without either of them exchanging a word of any significance. And it was necessary to talk soon, before they returned home, in case Ray tried to slough him off when he was back with his family and friends. Would he do that? Tim doubted it, though it was possible. A sense of shame might make him. He was determined not to let him slink out of it, not after last night.

What on earth had driven Ray to reveal himself? Sexual frustration? Something more than that, probably. Was he, too, going through a great crisis? It ought to be easier for Ray: he had no religious problems. Were there problems of which Tim had no inkling? The Spanish thing, virility; if you could not produce sons—he remembered something in Hemingway—people said you had no cojones. No balls, no spunk. Was it that? Or because he was so far in with Aaron and his crowd that there was no going back on the role he'd chosen to act? Yet now he had complicated matters for himself; he'd shown Tim what he was.

He was sure Ray was still awake. If only he could fall asleep himself, then there would be no decision, no sin, tonight at least: he might then feel easier in his mind, tomorrow. But sleep would not come.

'Tim! Are you awake? Tim!'

He would not answer. It was so easy not to. 'Yes,' he heard himself whisper.

'Come in with me tonight.'

'No.'

'Why not?'

Because I don't want to was all he needed to say. 'You come here.'

Ray silently moved his sleeping-bag and undid the zips.

CHAPTER SIX

Anthony dashed up the stairs, leaned back against the wall, and closed his eyes. The pistol hung from his right hand. 'You must all go,' he said, wearily. 'At once. I need this place now.'

'Why? What's happened?'

'I'm escaping arrest. There's a warrant signed by Sir Thomas Fairfax himself.'

'But the proclamation said no prisoners, no hostages!' Tim cried.

'I shall speak to him,' said Saint-Hill. The others looked at him: the idea was ridiculous.

'What crime have you committed?' Jake asked.

'Hoarding food. Selling it at exorbitant prices for personal profit. It's not true, of course. A gross exaggeration.'

There was an awkward silence, then Saint-Hill burst out: 'I shall speak to the Governor all the same!'

'Don't be a fool. Go on, get out, all of you.' He waved his pistol at them. 'Tim, bring me something to eat this evening. And . . . my music, and my lute. If it's still there.'

'What do you mean, if it's still there?'

'Fairfax's men have wrecked the place. I don't know what they thought they'd find.'

'Have they guessed where you are?'

'No.'

There was another silence; Anthony frowned, lost in his own thoughts. Jake went downstairs; Tim and Saint-Hill followed, more slowly. 'I think it's safe,' Jake said when they were outside. He shut the door of the tower and locked it, then gave the key to Tim.

'Where will you stay now?' Saint-Hill asked. 'Out of the question to return to the gatehouse. In any case, the new administration will want it for their soldiers. You're welcome to stay with me.'

'Or me,' said Jake.

The two men argued over this for a while, somewhat to Tim's amusement, for Saint-Hill was becoming quite waspish; then they asked him to choose, rather like two small boys squabbling over the one child left to make up one or other side in a game. 'I'll go with Jake,' he said.

Saint-Hill stumped off. Jake led the way through a maze of courts and alleys to a part of the city that was strange to Tim, arriving eventually outside an old half-timbered house in Parliament Street (prudently named, Tim thought) which was said to be the narrowest street in the world. 'This is home,' Jake said. 'The family business. We are in the cloth trade, or were, in better times.' Tim was impressed. The house, though little, was cheerful and well-furnished: it had an air of being looked after and loved. At the back was a neat garden, its walls covered in creepers which were a mass of autumnal reds and browns.

In the parlour sat a woman, sewing. 'My wife, Frances,' Jake said.

They ate very frugally; this family had not been hoarding food, though the two young daughters, who came in from playing just before the meal was served, did not appear at all starved. Some people, Frances said, had been

driven to eating their cats and dogs before the city surrendered, but they must have been extremely profligate in
the management of their households. Jake and his wife,
Tim discovered during the course of the evening, supported
neither party: they were, by natural inclination, Royalist,
but they had become sick of the errors of the King's government, and though they felt they could never support the
aims of Parliament, they hoped for fairer justice and
honesty under the new regime. Jake, finding time lay
heavily on his hands as the cloth trade had declined dramatically because of the war, had busied himself with a
number of minor jobs such as the sextonship of Holy
Trinity: a post left suddenly vacant and unfilled, like a
hundred others, when the King's men had occupied the
city after the previous siege. 'Where are those men now?'
He was referring to Lord Goring and his cavalry. 'Like the
army of King Cambysses they vanished without trace.
Swallowed up, perhaps, in the bogs of Dartmoor.'

'Vanished to their homes, more like,' Tim said. 'Those
that could.'

'What do you intend to do, now you are no longer
required at the gatehouse?'

'I don't know.' He had not thought about it. 'Leave
Exeter, probably.'

'Where will you go?'

'I don't know.' He saw himself, in his mind's eye, travelling alone in the middle of a straight dusty track that
stretched to the horizon, his belongings wrapped in a
bundle on his shoulders.

'You're welcome to stay here for a while.' Polite and
friendly though the invitation was, it did not sound very
pressing.

'Thank you. I will for tonight, if I may.'

It was growing dark. Frances lit candles. They gleamed in the pewter, made the ceiling beams flicker, cast strange shadows on faces. Tim felt comfortable, but he knew he had to go back to the tower of Holy Trinity.

Jake, as if he was reading Tim's thoughts, said 'It should be safe now. There's food in the kitchen; take it to him.'

He didn't love Aaron any more. He was quite certain of it; it was a fact like the truth blazed by the lightning on the Damascus road. He was free! The spell had broken; the dog's tail had lost a tin.

Afterwards, after Ray had gone, guilt then, the other tin. The clammy damp on his skin. But this knowledge: he did not love Aaron. Never again would he fall for someone so hopelessly out of reach. He was free!

He found his way by moonlight. The gatehouse was deserted and sinister; he did not want to go in, even though Anthony had asked for his music and his lute. He approached the church tower, afraid, listening for noises. A dog howled, outside the walls, in the ruins by the Quaker meeting-place. A window banged shut. Leaves rustled in the wind.

Footsteps: several men, walking purposefully. He shrank into the shadows cast by a buttress. There were three men. They stopped by the door of the tower, tried the handle, and expressed no surprise on finding it locked. One of them drew a pistol and fired, kicked it open. Running feet on the stairs, angry voices. Tim put down his basket of food against the church wall and moved as silently as he could to the door. The words, echoing in the spiral staircase, were quite clear.

'Are you Anthony Fare?'

97

'No.'

Someone laughed. 'He obviously is; bring him away.'

'Why?'

'You know the charge. The Governor wants to question you.'

'The Governor?'

'Or one of his officers, perhaps.'

A third voice said 'Don't cause us any trouble, sir. It's not a hanging offence, so kindly drop the pistol.'

'Don't come any nearer!'

There was a pause, then a rush across the room, shouts, blows from fists, another explosion. Someone fell heavily to the floor. After a moment's silence one of the intruders said 'Died, while resisting arrest.'

'Serve him right.'

Tim was horrified. *Anthony!* He had difficulty restraining himself from running up the stairs, demanding explanations, hurling abuse.

'Who fired the gun?'

'*He* did. In the fight. It went off accidentally.'

'What shall we do with him?'

'Leave him till morning. Send a report to the castle.'

Feet descending. Tim fled into the shadows. The three men hurried past, and ran down the steps into South Street. Tim waited, his heart thumping violently. He wanted to go into the tower, but he was frightened. Suppose the men returned? Eventually he found the courage, and there, in the moonlight, was Anthony, lying on his back in the middle of the floor. There was blood from a wound in the temple. Tim felt for the heart: nothing.

He was my friend. No, not really; that was self-deception. He would have betrayed me if he'd felt it necessary, used me to save himself. He was involved in murky business, no

98

doubt of it. A soldier of fortune. Someone trying to extract the most from the war to feather his own nest. Perhaps. These were only guesses; Tim had never grown near discovering what the real Anthony was like. He hadn't been unreasonable to work for, at times had seemed the most fascinating of men. But that was drink and talk, the warmth of a shared room. He was handsome and tall, and now he was dead: the blue eyes dead.

'You cannot blame the authorities,' Jake said, gently. 'It was not intended, I'm sure. Tomorrow we'll see if we can remove his possessions. Would you like to have his lute?'

'Yes. Yes, I would.'

'Did you love him?'

'No.'

'I thought you did.'

'I thought I did. For a while. But I did not.'

Tim woke early from a fitful sleep. Hunger had disturbed him often during the night, and he had felt, more than once, that it would be impossible to survive another day without food. His stomach gnawed and clutched, crying out against the situation which would not allow it to function normally. He was weak in all his limbs, as if he had a mild fever. The others were restless too; Aaron twitched and protested, and John and Ray from time to time muttered incomprehensible but apparently urgent, important words.

There was something changed about the quality of the light outside. He crawled over Aaron's body and opened the tent-flaps. The sun! Only then did he realize: their imprisonment was over! The cloud was still there, but it had lifted considerably; he could see, could see the way off Glaramara, for on that mountain, he now knew, they had spent the last three nights. He identified Great End. The cloud swirled; the crags disappeared and the sunlight darkened, but it did not matter: instead he saw into Borrowdale. Then the sun came again, and for a moment the clouds parted completely and there was the shining rocky peak of Bowfell, splendid and beautiful against the blue sky.

'Wake up! Wake up!'

'What's the matter? What is it?'

'The weather! There's sun; we can go! We're saved!'

They roused themselves instantly and peered out. 'Thank God,' Ray said.

There was no need to discuss what to do. They dressed, drank some water, packed their things. The tent was dismantled.

'Whose turn for it?' Aaron asked.

'Mine.' Tim shouldered it.

'He can't take a full shift,' Ray said. 'None of us can. We're not strong enough now.'

John agreed. 'Half an hour each today.'

'The holiday's over,' Tim said. 'Isn't it? Langdale, and then our mothers. We were going to climb Helvellyn, Scafell Pike, and Skiddaw.' No-one spoke. 'Well, another time perhaps.'

'Yes,' Ray said, and Aaron nodded.

They set off. John had been right about the direction when he had laid out the stones; he was still right when they came to the marsh. Now, of course, they could see the way round it, could see, in fact, how obvious was the route from Glaramara to the Langdale–Wasdale motorway, even though there was no track and the ground was rough and uneven. Progress was slow. It was not the confident stride of the four fit young colts who had easily conquered Great Gable on Saturday evening; it was more the dull leaden plod of aged carthorses, stumbling through weakness. Tim, burdened by the tent, was particularly slow. Ray walked with him.

John and Aaron gradually moved ahead, and, when they were some distance off, Ray said 'At last we can talk.'

'There's a lot to talk about,' Tim replied, laughing. 'Quite a lot!'

Ray was silent, embarrassed a little, not knowing where to begin. 'When I was thirteen, no, just fourteen . . . yes, it was in the third year . . . Ron used to come round to the flat on Saturday mornings. We'd look at these magazines, nude women and that, and . . . I don't remember exactly how it began . . . we . . . we both . . .'

'Ron! You and *Ron*?' Tim was amazed. It was almost a stab of pain: jealousy.

'I know you fancy him.'

'I . . . did.' He recovered himself, pretended to look nonchalant. 'Was this . . . often?'

'I can't remember. I don't know how many times. It wasn't for long; I mean, Ron, he was just shy of girls, and the same went for me . . . I mean, I thought it did. Anyway, it stopped, and we started going out with girls. Well, most of the boys were going out with girls. Our friends. You know, mates, a gang. I didn't . . . I just didn't enjoy it, though I kidded myself I was having fun. I mean I knew inside I was different, right from the start, but it was a feeling I pushed away. Perhaps I hadn't met a girl I really liked, I said. But it wasn't; I mean I know when Ron and I stopped I was really cut up about it. It was Ron finished it of course; he'd met this Philippa somebody, and I thought, oh well, maybe it was just a phase. Ron had grown out of it quicker than me, that was all. Then, last year, there was you.'

'*Me?*'

'You'd always been on your own, and people said you were . . . well . . . wet . . . and queer . . . and I told myself I didn't like you at all in the fourth and fifth forms. I suppose because nobody did. I'm sorry. I mean I never really thought why. I'm sorry, Tim. But last year . . . you were staring at nothing, one day. At a brick wall. You looked so sad. Sad! I wanted to put my arms round you and say, it's all right! I was shocked. By what I felt, I mean. I thought everything out after that. Put all the pieces together. And I knew it was boys . . . men. Pictures of men in magazines, they really stir me, not like those female nudes of Ron's. I never told anyone. How could I? Ron, all my other friends, the first eleven crowd . . . well! I couldn't lose them. I'd have nothing.'

'You could have told me.'

'I wish I had. I mean, I knew you were; it's obvious—'

'Obvious?'

'I don't mean you're a pansy, or some freak; it's because you never go with girls, and the way you look at Ron. But I just couldn't tell you. You didn't fancy me; that was quite plain. I thought you'd be annoyed probably, and that would be worse, being rejected, much worse than if I never told you. But . . . this week. It was *awful* when you insisted on coming, and Ron said it was all right with him. I tried to persuade him to change his mind . . . do you remember? . . . I'm sorry. Then all the pretence of chasing that girl from the youth hostel! Stupid. Then you . . . in the same tent. I struggled and struggled and I thought I'd burst . . . like some gas cylinder exploding. And I seduced you. Is that what it was? I'd have exploded otherwise, gone berserk. I'd got to that stage it didn't matter any longer you might hate me; well, it mattered less than the fact that I had to do something.'

'Ray.' He tried to sound as gentle as he could. 'I don't . . . I can't love you.'

'I don't love you either. I don't think that's the word for it. I just . . . fancy you. Is that terrible?'

'These past few days! The weather, and being shut up in the tent, and thinking we'd starve to death! All that and it's seemed less than . . . well, it's been a crisis for me, too. A civil war. If you'd tried it only three nights back, I'd have kicked you out. Sinful and wicked. Catholicism, you see.'

'I know. That's another reason I never said before.'

'I may be coming to terms with it. I don't know. I've got to be me!'

'That's it exactly! We've *got* to be *us*! Losing Ron, the others . . . it may not matter so much. Well, it does matter, but perhaps it's not so important. I can't go on being a fraud. A pretend-man.'

'Pretend-man?' Tim smiled. 'That's just the word I call myself!'

'Called. Not now.'

'Yes. Or I hope so. It won't be easy.'

'For neither of us, I guess. Do you . . . do you want us to go on seeing each other, when we get back?'

'Of course I do! I want to know you, more than anybody else I've ever met!'

'But are you ashamed . . . of what we've done?'

'I ought to be. But, now, at this moment . . . no.'

'Would you . . . will there . . . be another time?'

'Don't. Don't ask things like that. I don't know. Wrong on two counts. Sinful and wicked. And I don't love you. But I was happy, Ray. I can't work that out yet. Someone . . . wanting me. Being needed. I suddenly knew I mattered, to myself as well as you. I was a real person.'

'You must come home. Tomorrow, or the day after. And

meet my parents. You'd like them! They're great people.'

'I'd love to.'

'I'm . . . oh, happy!'

'I'm on the road to being happy. I think.' Why could he not love Ray, he asked himself. Ray wasn't ugly. A real man. Was it that he was too soft? Too confused? It was going to be, ultimately, someone quite different. Someone much more all of a piece, more sure of things, who could say: if you want me we'll make a marvellous life, and if you don't, I shan't break my heart. Someone whose personality was more like John's. Not John, of course. That would be quite absurd! Never again would he let himself become infatuated with a boy who wasn't his own kind. That would be a recipe for disaster and despair. But, one day, years off perhaps, there might be a man along the lines of John.

'They're waiting for us,' Ray said.

Why should he think that? He didn't like the idea of being deferred to, coddled, turned into a substitute woman. He wanted to be bossed around, fall in with the other person's whims and wishes. Not ill-treated, certainly, simply needed in a strong kind of way, not be enmeshed in a soft fuzzy web of sentiment. Or was this, he wondered, a kind of running away from emotion?

'I'll take the tent!' Aaron shouted. The first generous action he's ever indulged in, Tim thought.

'It's all right!' Ray shouted back. 'My turn!'

'It isn't,' Tim said.

'I know. If I take it we don't have to catch them up.' Aaron shrugged his shoulders, his most characteristic gesture. John and he walked on, up the pass. 'Method in my madness,' Ray said.

They were silent for a while, Ray getting used to the

burden of the tent. Tim felt its weight becoming intolerable, yet on that first day it had not seemed too irksome. It was the hunger, the total listlessness in the limbs, the lightness in the head. Mountain walking, even though it meant they could now reach safety, was the most wretched pastime imaginable.

There was still a mass of low cloud, breaking up and reforming in the wind. But shafts of sunlight pierced it, revealing scree and crag, muttering rivulets of water drizzling down rock. They could see far enough, and the way was obvious. Around them, grass, bracken dying, the mud and stones of the track. The top of the pass was only minutes away.

'There's places at home where people like us meet,' Ray said.

'Are there?' Tim was surprised. He'd never heard of such a thing.

'A pub. And some group that meets in somebody's house.'

'I'd be terrified.'

'Why?'

'I just would, I'm sure. What would they want of me, I'd be wondering.'

'They're people like anybody else.'

'I'd still be frightened. How did you find this out?'

'You know that effeminate boy, Noel Haynes? Well, he is; he must be. I once looked inside his desk. I was going past his classroom after school one day, and I thought . . . I just wondered if there might be something interesting, to confirm that he was. Well, there was this newspaper. I took it home and read it, every page of it, every line, then had a hell of a job smuggling it back. There was this guide in it, all the pubs and places in England where gay people meet.

Anyway . . . I want to go to this pub at home. I don't think I'd dare go in by myself, though. Will you . . . come with me?'

'I don't know. I'll think about it.'

'Nobody's going to *rape* you, Tim!'

'Why do you want to go there?'

'To meet others like us, of course! You can't live in a vacuum!'

'What else was in this paper?'

'Oh, articles, reviews, stories about queer-bashing, lovers being arrested by the police. All kinds of oppression. Adverts . . . lonely people wanting to contact other lonely people.'

'What if you met somebody in this pub you know, someone who's not . . . ?'

'I don't care. I've decided not to care.'

'They might be, well, very strange. The men who go to this pub.'

'Look, we can't be the only two nice decent homosexuals in the world!'

'I suppose not.' He had a cheering vision of hundreds of happy uncomplicated people enjoying themselves together, sharing each others' lives. 'I suppose not.'

'I've come a long distance, these past few days. You said it was civil war, and that's very true. I've been imagining I was in the Alcázar all the time in the tent, an Alcázar of guys like me. Odd. Besieged by my own side, la República.'

'Have you!' Tim looked at him intently.

'Yes, a long distance.' He stumbled and nearly fell. 'I only hope I get there.' He sat down, suddenly, on a boulder.

'Here, let me have the tent.'

'No, no, I'll be OK. Give Ron a yell. It's his turn.'

'They're out of sight, over the top of the pass.'

'Let's rest a minute.' They stared up at the grim north face of Great End, slowly emerging through the cloud. 'We're not in trim,' Ray panted. 'I'm aching all over! Not just the walk. Several nights in a sleeping-bag . . . not like my bed at home.'

Would he go to this pub with Ray? Wild horses wouldn't drag him in there alone. It was a perfectly reasonable thing to do, but . . . He tried to nudge out of his mind pictures of the altar at church, of Father Sullivan, of the host at Mass. Would he go to Confession this Saturday? He wasn't sure that he had the courage. And he wasn't sure, if he did, that he would be quite honest.

He took the tent from Ray, and helped him to his feet. 'Some time,' Ray said, 'I shall tell my parents.' Tim looked blank. 'About me, what I am.'

'What!'

'I want them to know.'

'They'd chuck you out of the house!'

'Would yours?'

'I'm bloody sure they would!'

'They can't love you very much, then.'

'What do you mean?'

'If they really love you they'll accept what you are. They may not like it . . . but they're your parents!'

'They'd never accept it. Never. I'd never tell them. They'd be so hurt.'

'What's better, a lifetime of lies and pretence?'

'I don't *want* a lifetime of lies and pretence. But I'd lose them if they found out. I know I would! My mother would say I was trying to kill her; my father would say I was hopelessly vile and corrupt.'

'They don't sound very nice.' That might well be true, Tim thought, but it was his prerogative to make that kind of judgement. It annoyed him to hear such a comment. 'Mine are all right,' Ray went on. 'I mean, they're good to me, don't ask prying questions all the time, let me do what I like. More or less. We can talk about most things. I expect they imagine I sleep with girls occasionally; my father gave me a wink the morning after I'd come in once at two a.m. from a party. I don't suppose he was that innocent when he got married! No, there's only one thing they'd really loathe: if I stopped being Spanish.'

'What do you mean?'

'Stopped *feeling* like a Spaniard, I suppose. It's difficult to explain. Turned into a cold East Anglian or something.'

'You mean not speaking Spanish, not eating their food?'

'More than that. Anyway . . . I think my mother would accept . . . me.'

'I can't believe it!'

'It would take some doing, even so. My father . . . I don't know. Some Spanish men, they . . . they have this strong family thing, about having sons. He wouldn't like it. But I'm sure he'd wish me luck.'

'They must be remarkable people. Completely exceptional.'

'I don't see why. Maybe yours are the exceptions.'

They were at the top of the pass. Below them a great sweep of land: Angle Tarn just down from where they stood a brown and green landscape away to the left and ahead, and in the distance, like crouching lions, the two Langdale mountains, Harrison Stickle and the Pike of Stickle. To the right, the majestic rocky wall of Bowfell. John and Aaron were by the tarn, and, coming to meet them, was a line of men, struggling over Rossett Pike. A rescue party! Already there were shouts, hands waving. John and Aaron stopped.

'Tim: I think I'm going to faint!'

'No, no, you're not. Lean on me.'

Slowly they began the descent. By Angle Tarn all was clamour and confusion. The Mountain Rescue were overjoyed; they hadn't held much hope of finding the boys alive. They clustered round, asking excited questions: Tim stared, bewildered, at their great rucksacks, their equipment, ropes, stretchers, first aid. They, in turn, were equally astonished. There seemed nothing wrong with these lads, not even a few broken limbs. All they wanted was food. Soon the four of them were eating ham rolls and mint-cake, and drinking hot coffee.

'I'm going to faint,' Ray whispered. And did so. The men leapt into action, glad that their equipment was justified, and Ray was revived, placed on a stretcher and covered with a blanket. The boys' rucksacks were taken, and someone picked up the tent. All four should be carried down on stretchers, the leader insisted. Tim thought this excessive, absurdly melodramatic, but he did as he was told. Aaron, too, complied, but John flatly refused. The argument was quite heated. He was perfectly capable of walking, he said; just because he hadn't eaten for two days didn't mean he was a hospital case. So they let him walk.

From the stretcher, crags, waterfalls, sheep and bracken seemed disconnected, floating in space. Tim couldn't relate one thing to another; this, and the swaying motion, made him feel sick. He'd be better on foot, he thought, but it was too late now. He'd abdicated, handed himself over to other people's responsibility. John was just ahead of him: a pretty impressive person, Tim decided.

The men carrying the stretcher kept asking questions. Tim told them the gist of what had happened: there wasn't, really, much to say. 'What did you do all that time?' he was asked. 'Four of you cooped up in that tent. Weren't you bored stiff?'

'No.' He smiled. 'We got to know each other very well. That's all.'

CHAPTER SEVEN

He wondered if it was officially closed to visitors, but no virger came down the aisle to turn him out. In the crossing sat the members of a choir and an orchestra, pausing for a moment in their rehearsal for tomorrow's performance of the B minor Mass. The conductor was discussing a detail with the first violinist. Otherwise it was as it might have been centuries ago, the same pillars, the same superb vault at which Fairfax's soldiers would have gazed. Not a trace of the hideous wall remained, and the organ—the successor to the one despoiled by the New Model—was all that now separated nave from quire. His guide-book said that the Princess Henrietta Maria had been baptized here in 1644, and the font, an elegant and unpretentious piece of seventeenth-century workmanship, looked as if it dated from then, was perhaps made specially for that inauspicious occasion. It was disappointing, however, to read that it was first used in 1687, disappointing also to realize that there was nothing of interest, even in this building, that had lasted from the Civil War. But, unlike Holy Trinity and the south gate, it was not a so-called progress that had rubbed out memory; it was the opposite: a desire to preserve and enhance the beauty of one of the world's great master-pieces.

The conductor tapped his baton, and the choir rose. It was the closing chorus of Bach's *Gloria*: cum Sancto Spiritu in gloria Dei Patris. A blaze of sound! A five-part fugue so quick and light on its feet that its rhythm alone would have danced the glory of God, but voices, instruments, the soaring columns of the cathedral itself did more than dance or sing; united in one joyous dazzling tapestry, in which the trumpets were bright stitches of gold and silver that looped it together, they *were* the glory of God.

Tim, moved to tears, stared at a truth he had just discovered: religion was not the dribbling of squalid secrets to a black-gowned ogre behind a grille (how many times?), not a set of prohibitions, briars that bound his joys and desires. It was this, a kind of ecstasy in which he was the trumpet while the music lasted, himself a part of God's glory. He had sensed it before, in the mountains in sunlight, but had not known what it was. Ray, when they met, would doubtless laugh at him, but he would have found something similar in Toledo, at the Alcázar, however differently he chose to name it.

Cum Sancto Spiritu in gloria Dei Patris. With the Holy Ghost, in the Glory of God the Father. Amen.

In Mickleden, the flat valley at the head of Langdale where heather and rough ground gave way to fields and hedges, Aaron made his stretcher-bearers stop. He threw off the blanket, sat up, and before anyone could object, he was standing. 'I shall look such a bloody fool being carried in on that!' he exclaimed. 'What do you imagine our mothers will say? Mine will go potty thinking I'm half dead!' The mothers, they had been told, would be waiting for them, at the Old Dungeon Ghyll Hotel. 'I'm going to walk!' he announced.

Tim and Ray agreed, and it was allowed. Ray could only just manage it, and Aaron limped, noticeably. 'It's a nail in my boot,' he said.

The Old Dungeon Ghyll was a hive of activity. There were newspaper reporters and a television crew, but the Mountain Rescue people pushed them aside, saying 'Not now, not now! Later!' to all their questions. John marched up to the bar and ordered a whisky and dry ginger.

The landlord poured it for him. 'On the house,' he said.

The mothers appeared. There was a tremendous hulla-balloo, tears, embraces, and amazement, like the Mountain Rescue team's, and their sons were not injured. People pressed into the bar, newspapermen, others who just wanted to stare. The landlord took the boys and their mothers through to his own quarters at the back of the hotel, and now, in privacy, out came the explanations: the history of the families' distress; the interest of the media and how irritating that had been at times, how helpful at others; how Mr Hewitt had arranged for the four women to travel at once to Ambleside. One of the Sunday papers wanted the exclusive rights to the story. 'There is no story,' Tim said, but Aaron told him to shut up. Mrs Hewitt had been a tower of strength, Mrs Keegan said, particularly as far as Mrs Brown was concerned: Aaron's mother had been in hysterics ever since she'd heard they were missing.

It all fell on Tim's ears like a torrent, a bewildering barrage in an alien language: he nodded his head, said yes and no in the right places, but, inside, he was filled with an acute sense of disappointment that the ordeal on the mountain was over. That, too, was bewildering, for he had had no intuition that this might be his reaction. Those long days and nights of yearning for food had passed; he was alive and safe, and here was one of the hotel staff putting a plate of bacon, egg, sausage, tomato, mushroom and fried bread in front of him, with toast and marmalade and coffee to follow: yet, in his mind, he was still in the tent on the inhospitable top of Glaramara, the four of them in a kind of friendship he had never known before and never would again, while outside the vast landscape and sky, mountain and cloud, cut them off from the rest of the world, held total sway, magnificent and terrifying.

A doctor came and examined them, and said they were remarkably fit, considering; all they needed was sleep. *Sleep?* Yes, he insisted, despite their protests; in a moment they would go upstairs and rest. After that they could talk to reporters and television interviewers if they wished. Then, Tim supposed, the tedious journey; to Ambleside to pick up their mothers' luggage, on to Penrith to catch the train, and by this evening he would be back in the dull grey East coast port with its uninteresting scenery and the uninteresting span of his life. Of course there would be changes. He had to grapple, alone, with the weight of majority opinion, and two thousand years of religious tradition. And he would have to pick up the reins of school work, home, parents. What he feared most was that all he had gained in the tent would be lost: the self-discoveries and the resolutions would evaporate in the cold light of routine; the friendships formed would dilute in the ordinary patterns of life.

He talked with Mrs Suñer, Mrs Brown and Mrs Hewitt. Mrs Suñer and Mrs Brown had known each other for some time through the friendship between their sons; John had met both women, and Ray and Aaron had met Mrs Hewitt before: only he and his own mother were strangers. Mrs Brown had had little responsibility for her son's good looks: she was squat and plain, a talkative fussy pub landlady, obviously formidable with the customers at closing time, 'an old nag,' Aaron had said, rightly. She was giving Mrs Hewitt a lengthy history of Ron's previous escapades, much to his embarrassment; 'so much more of a lad for mischief than my other three!' Mrs Hewitt was quiet, like John; there was a great ease between them, a confidence and belief in each other that did not require much expression in words. What anxieties she had experienced they had all heard in those few memorable minutes on the radio; she felt no need to repeat herself. She was simply happy that all had turned out well; John was a young man of good sense whom she trusted implicitly. Ray and his mother jabbered non-stop in Spanish. Mrs Suñer, jet black hair and dark skin, shining dark eyes, looked older than she probably was: it was all emotion, excitement, exclamation, wild expansive gestures.

His own mother showed up worst, Tim thought. Despite the distress the women had shared, Mrs Keegan stood aloof from the friendship that had formed between the other three. It was a sort of snobbery. They were the wives of ordinary working men: a builder, a publican, a chef. Tim's father was a civil servant. Not that Mrs Keegan had anything to be snobbish about. Her parents, both of labouring stock, had emigrated to England because their house had been burned down in the civil war of 1922; Grandpa Casey had worked for a brewery in Cork and eventually drank himself to death in Ipswich. But Mrs Keegan, determined to succeed in the English middle class, had lost all her Irishness; not even the slightest trace of an accent remained. The millstone of Roman Catholicism was her only ancestral bequest to her son. She looked at her watch, yawned, drummed her fingers, and kept Aaron, John, and Ray at arm's length. She wanted to get back home as soon as possible, where she would doubtless issue a papal bull forbidding Tim to take part in such an expedition ever again.

The boys were sent upstairs to rest. Tim shared a room with Aaron.

'So a Sunday paper wants our story,' Aaron said, as he took off his clothes. 'Leave it to me. I'll screw a good sum of money out of them; don't worry.'

'Yes. All right.'

'John and Ray think it's OK if *I* do it. Split four ways equally, of course. Maybe I can get enough to buy some equipment for my group. Loudspeakers.'

'What group?'

'Aaron's Rod. I told you.'

'Oh. Yes.'

'Look. About Friday. We'll go to my place afterwards, shall we? Better than yours, really. We can drink as long as we like there; I mean it's a pub and Dad will let us. You can all stay the night too. Mum said.'

'Did my mother put you off?' Aaron did not answer. Tim slipped between the sheets. 'I don't know why we're going to bed at this hour of the day; I'm not a bit tired.' But in less than a minute he was fast asleep.

'I'm completely converted to the cause of Parliament,' Saint-Hill said, for the third time. 'My Royalist beliefs were nothing other than wild delusions. I thought the monarchy stood for all that was best in the English tradition, the protection of personal freedom. I was wrong.'

'I can't imagine how you thought King Charles represented freedom,' Tim said.

'Yes, yes, yes, I know, I know.' Saint-Hill was impatient. 'I simply regarded him as an aberration. I was thinking of

116

his father, and his father's illustrious predecessor, Queen Elizabeth.'

'What about her brother Edward? And Henry the Eighth, Henry the Seventh?'

Saint-Hill ignored this. 'The King has always been the symbol of justice, the guardian of his subjects' rights, the defender of their liberties. Of course there have been exceptions from time to time. Now I see that the symbol isn't just tarnished. It's smashed in pieces. But it has been replaced by something far better, a Parliament of freely elected men, who will allow us to return to the greatest liberty of all: quietly getting on with our own business.'

'You may be right.' It was certainly true, in Exeter at least, that the change to a Parliamentary administration was proving beneficial. There were, of course, some regrettable minor occurrences, such as Anthony's death, and the incident with the cathedral's organ pipes. But the conversion of the cathedral into two places of Dissenting worship was the only innovation the authorities had forced on the city churches. The clergy were allowed to keep their livings provided they were not too flagrant in their display of Laudian observances. The ringleader of the strange dance in Cathedral Yard had been put in the stocks for blasphemous conduct. The message, whispered abroad from Fairfax's headquarters in the castle, was that diligent and sober behaviour was the watchword; the citizens should act industriously and honestly and no-one would come to any harm. The most influential Royalist sympathisers, however, were brought in for questioning and were heavily fined, in order to stop them financing any further escapade that might be started on the King's behalf. All protested they were now ruined, though this was far from the truth.

Tim was walking about the streets with Saint-Hill, observing how rapidly things were returning to normal. Since the city had surrendered, trade was once again possible, and though supplies were still short, there was some food available, and prices had fallen dramatically. The first ships to arrive since the estuary had been cleared had docked that morning. Cargoes of coal, fresh fruit, flour and cheese were unloaded, and what little cloth the city had in store was transferred to the ships for export. Cows, sheep and pigs had earlier been driven in to market from distant towns and villages: business was brisk.

Neighbours, who for too long had not spoken to one another, now mingled freely; and the alehouses were busy, though in a discreet fashion: the distaste for strong drink in some quarters of the Parliament administration was well-known, and one of Fairfax's first orders was to treble the penalties for drunkenness. Sir Thomas, however, was not an extremist. He had over-ruled the wishes of some of his subordinates that the taverns should be closed indefinitely; such an action, he argued, would not help to bind up wounds. It was not his intention to alienate those who disliked Puritanism, but to win them over.

Saint-Hill led Tim into the White Hart, and observed, as they sipped from pewter mugs of beer, that it was quite remarkable that the supply of liquor in the city had not dried up altogether during the siege. This was probably because the alehouses had been so unfrequented; it was good to see people he had not met for months now daring to be sociable. 'What plans do you have in mind,' he asked, 'now your employment here is finished?'

'I don't know,' Tim confessed. 'There is nothing to hold me in Exeter. I had thought of leaving, but where or for what purpose I'm undecided.'

'Allow me to accompany you for a while,' said Saint-Hill. 'I'm leaving for Bristol shortly. I have relations there.'

'It would be a pleasure. Thank you.'

'The way is long when one travels alone.'

In the afternoon they continued their stroll. Workmen were repairing a pump in Catherine Street that had been allowed to fall into disuse some weeks before; a baker in St Martin's Lane was painting his shop-front; middens were being cleared near St Stephen's. In the cathedral, however, labourers had already set about the task of building the wall at the crossing: it mutilated, hideously, the beauty and harmonious shape of the interior. The New Model soldiers were much in evidence, at the gates and in the busier streets, but an acquaintance of Saint-Hill's, whom they met in Butchers' Row, told them that the bulk of the army would be withdrawn tomorrow or the next day, in order to speed up the liberation of the remaining areas of the West Country still in Royalist hands. Fairfax himself was to command them, leaving the government of the city to civilians, who would be protected by a small garrison stationed at the castle.

'We might as well think about departing ourselves,' said Saint-Hill.

'Yes, perhaps we should,' Tim answered.

'But in the opposite direction.'

Next morning they set out, Tim on Anthony Fare's white horse. He had with him Anthony's lute; he had asked for it at the gatehouse and the soldiers who fetched it did not question why he wanted it. They travelled at a moderate pace; having no pressures on them of any sort there was no need to hurry. Soon they were surrounded by the quiet of the autumn fields. The day was warm and sunny, but with a hint that frost would occur by nightfall.

It was a rich, lush countryside they travelled through, of water-meadows and orchards, but there were signs everywhere in unpicked fruit and rotting crops that husbandry had been neglected, and deserted villages and burned-out barns showed that armies had trampled across the land, first advancing then retreating, again and again, during these past few years of war.

Saint-Hill waxed eloquent on every subject imaginable, though always turning back to politics, religion, or military matters; some of his discourse was, as always, too enthusiastic, but often it contained a certain shrewdness. Tim laughed at his most elaborate flights of fancy, and, though Saint-Hill knew he was being mocked, he did not complain. He was a man without malice, whose feelings were invariably generous, but whose ideas were never wholly consistent. He was soft and vulnerable, in need of protection, almost a Don Quixote. But he shortened the way admirably; as they neared Taunton, late in the evening, Tim thought to himself that the time could not have passed more quickly or more pleasantly.

It was a month later and he was alone, in the mountains. The air was sharp, the light brilliant, the sky a dazzling blue. All around him soared crags and peaks of incomparable majesty. In their highest gullies the year's first snow lay, blinding in the sun. He reined in his horse and observed warily. The young man, who was resting on the bank of the lake, stood up, walked down to the water, and began to wash his face. He was the most handsome person Tim had ever seen: tall, slim, with a slow, almost languid walk that seemed to conceal reserves of strength. His face was sunburned and his hair the colour of flax. Tim dismounted and led his horse; the young man, hearing the movement, looked up, but went back to his washing. Eventually he turned round and stared.

'Stranger?' he asked.

'Yes.'

'Looking for work?'

'Yes.'

'There's plenty to be done. Where are you from?'

'I set out from Exeter four weeks ago.'

'Exeter! That's far away. Another world! Is it for the King, or Parliament?'

'Exeter? Whether it is for either is a question no-one's asked, but to answer yours, it surrendered to Fairfax a while since.'

'And you? No, there's no need to tell me. The war is almost over and the King has lost. Some say he's already in France. What did you see on your journey?'

'In the towns much is normal, except where the battle was severe, as in Taunton or Bristol or Gloucester. In parts of the countryside there is such desolation as I never thought to dream of. Land wasted by foraging armies, cows wandering the highroads bellowing for their masters, blackened farmsteads, beggars by the dozen, men crippled or blinded, motherless children: all victims of war, or caught in the cross-fire of it.'

'I have a farm that I never thought to inherit so early in life. My father was killed at Naseby; my mother died from a stray shot one morning when she was feeding the hens. An accident, yes, but no-one stopped long enough to discuss it.' He bent down, drank from the water, and wiped his mouth. 'There is a deal of work to be done. Fields overgrown with weeds, animals to be fed, thatch to repair, cooking and cleaning. You can help me if you wish.'

'I would like to.'

'You may not when you see the state of things.'

'Are you married?'

'No. Nor do I intend to be. Are you?'

'No.' They looked at each other for a moment.

'Do these mountains please you?'

'There's . . . grandeur, solitude. They're beautiful. A man could be utterly lost, yet find himself here.'

'I was born here, in Wasdale. What is your name?'

'Tim.'

'Mine is John.'

'It's a name I like.'

'I'll show you the farm.' The war had not left this remote place untouched. The house was a ruin; most of the windows had been smashed and part of the roof burned. 'It is largely derelict,' John said. 'The rain has soaked into all the bedrooms and they cannot be used, and downstairs only the kitchen is habitable. Can you thatch a roof?'

'I can learn.'

'Good.'

'I'll start in here.' Tim surveyed the kitchen: piles of unwashed dishes, half-eaten food, a blocked sink, a smoking fire. 'I can cook.'

'I have little or no money, but we can share everything, if that suits you.'

'It will.'

'I'll start outside, then. Your coming gives me some hope: the farm will benefit first, and, afterwards, we shall too.'

Later, having eaten, they sat on either side of a warm fire that did not smoke now, puffing at pipes of tobacco, in a companionable silence.

'I don't know how long I shall stay,' Tim said. He was

fingering the strings of Anthony's lute, trying to work out chords.

'No? Well, you are right not to tie yourself down. We're young; you will want to see the world yet, as I shall myself.'

'Yes.'

'Let us see how it works. There's a little beer left in the cellar; we'll drink to our success.' He went out and fetched it. 'That fire's good,' he said when he returned. 'How did you manage it?'

'I swept the chimney. It had not been done for centuries.'

'I'll bring the mattress up to the hearth and we can sleep in the warm. Does that suit you too?'

'Yes.'

'I've dreamed about it,' Aaron said. 'Every single night.' They were sitting round the fire in the bar of his father's pub, The King's Head. It was long after closing time and all the other customers had gone. Mr and Mrs Brown were in the kitchen making cocoa. Tim had enjoyed his glimpse of the family. Peter was shy and silent, and though he was obviously Aaron's younger brother, he was not nearly so good-looking. Mr Brown was as Ron had described him, genial and easy-going; he had a pleasant casual friendship with his sons, obviously liked and trusted them a lot. Tim had not expected this; he was now so used to feeling Ron was not a person to be trusted. However, it was quite usual, he thought, with people you knew at school to find their behaviour at home was different from what you imagined. Though this had not been true at the Suñers two days ago. Of the two elder brothers there was no sign; David was married and had his own house, and Martin, an art student, was at his girl-friend's.

'Have you heard any more from the newspaper?' Ray asked.

'If you'd been around yesterday or the day before you'd know,' Aaron replied. 'They want three thousand words on the subject by a fortnight tomorrow. Who's going to do it?'

'Tim,' John suggested. 'University potential, and all that.'

'I don't mind,' Tim said.

'Good. That's settled, then,' Aaron decided. 'And don't forget to name the idiot who lost the compass.'

'How much are they paying?' Ray asked.

'A hundred pounds.'

'A hundred pounds! That's marvellous!'

'You're joking! It's not exactly what Harold Wilson got for his memoirs, is it? And we're not train robbers' wives, or Raquel Welch.'

'You haven't quite the same attractions, Ron.'

'I told them it was peanuts, and I wouldn't do it for less than five hundred. But they just laughed. Still, it's something, I suppose. It'll help towards the loud-speakers. My share, that is.'

'Twenty-five each,' John said. 'Not bad!'

'Where have you all been this past couple of days?' Aaron asked, irritably. 'There's me slaving my guts out getting you money, and no sign of any of you. *You* might have shown up, Ray! I phoned you last night, but your mother said you were out.'

'I was. How far did you get with Mary Miller?'

'Mind your own business.' He helped himself to a cigarette, then offered them round. 'Where were you last night, Ray?'

'I went out for a drink. With Tim.'

'Oh.' Aaron was a little surprised. 'And the night before?'

'I should tell *you* to mind your own business. Tim came to supper, if you really must know.' Ray blushed, for John was looking at him too. Aaron would now have doubts about Ray, Tim thought, or, at least, Aaron would say he had doubts. Was he on the turn, that sort of thing. He'd discussed this with Ray last night. A week ago, Ray said, he would have crawled into a hole and died if he'd been the recipient of such a comment, particularly from Ron. Now it was not quite so important, though he wouldn't like it, of course. It was inevitable, however, that Aaron would find out eventually, but at least one thing had come clear during the days in the tent: he was more tolerant than Ray had thought. How so, Tim asked. See how he treats you, Ray answered; he doesn't really care if you are as long as he's not pestered himself.

The evening at the Suñers had been fascinating. The grandparents were like withered old nuts, the dark skin of their oval-shaped faces unbelievably creased; the same jet black hair and dark eyes as the rest of the family. They spoke English only with difficulty. Ray's father was a thin wiry man who chain-smoked, physically quite different from his son, less heavy, not so tough. The whole evening had been a plunge into a completely foreign world for Tim. Politics, religion, and Spain dominated the conversation, though Mrs Suñer frequently asked them not to discuss these wearisome topics, tonight at least; it was so boring for Ramón's friend. Mr Suñer, after several requests, produced his guitar. He was an expert, or, at least, Tim thought so. Ron would like to learn this kind of thing, Ray said, but he hadn't the patience. There followed an hour of flamenco, and songs: the melancholic songs of the losing side, young men tragically killed in battle. Then it was Ray's turn; pieces by Pedrell, Turina, de Falla. He was not as good as his father, perhaps never would be: music did not flow with the same grace and ease from his finger-tips. But Tim was surprised. He had not known that Ray played the guitar at all. Several times he had to remind himself that he was in a council flat in his home town of England: there was Daz on the shelf, an English gas-cooker, Sainsbury's tea-bags in the pot. They had eaten English chicken and chips. He was not in Castile, or Galicia, or Andalusia.

Last night he and Ray had visited the gay pub. They had gone in with beating hearts and nervous shivers. It turned out to be rather an anticlimax: it was so ordinary. Nothing about the people in there, apart from some fragments of conversation they overheard, indicated that they were different from the rest of the world. He wondered what he had been expecting. Handbags and make-up? Limp-wristed drag queens? Something, perhaps, that would upset him so much that he would say, no, he was wrong; it wasn't the life for him. No-one accosted them, though several people eyed them with a certain curiosity. There's nothing, he thought, to prevent him coming in again.

He came back to the conversation round the fire; Aaron was wondering what would have happened if they hadn't lost their way on Glaramara. Tim found his glass had been refilled.

'We'd have had a much more enjoyable holiday in some ways,' John said. 'But less to remember.'

'I didn't not enjoy it,' Aaron said. 'In retrospect. Seen Lesley?'

'Of course.'

'That's why you haven't been around.'

'Yes.'

'Done anything interesting?'

'Catching up. There was a lot to talk about.'

'I wonder if they do,' Tim murmured to Ray.

'Who? What?'

'John and Lesley.'

'After three years? Bit crazy not to. Though John will never say. A very private person, John.'

So are we all, Tim thought. How complicated it is! I'm coming to terms with it, slowly. The next few years will be the aftermath of civil war, mending the parts that bleed. Will I be happy? There's a chance, even though growing up's so painful. There will be a time when it all slots into place; there must be. Then I shall be free: I've already chosen to be what I am, which is what I always have been.